Th[illegible] in the Bush

By Pamela Ann Sheppard

Pajent Publishing

P. A. SHEPPARD: THE BODY IN THE BUSH

Cover Art by iStock

Oxley District is a fictional place in West Sussex. It has three main towns – Great Oxing, Nunsfield and Oxmouth.

Chapter One

The first hint of trouble was the metallic blue Fiat parked in front of Indigo's garage. She gave a weary sigh. The only reason her sister would be calling on her at three thirty in the morning was if she had a problem. It was the last thing she needed tonight. She'd spent three weeks trawling the backstreets of London looking for her latest teenage runaway, six hours persuading the fourteen-year-old to return home, two hours driving from London to the South Coast, and the best part of another three hours trying to extract herself from the clutches of Chloe's grateful parents. All she really wanted was to drop into her bed and sleep until noon. For a moment, she seriously considered continuing down the road and finding a Bed and Breakfast place to flop in. Then common sense reasserted itself and she pulled in beside the Fiat.

She sat for a moment, gathering the last remnants of her energy, then got out of the car and slammed the door. A bevy of birds immediately fluttered up from the dark mass of overhanging trees. Indigo crunched across the gravel of her roadside driveway and made her way down along the sloping earth path that led to the tiny converted railway station she called home. A few feet from the bottom, a small dark shape slunk out from the undergrowth and wrapped itself about her ankles, impeding progress.

"Hello Midnight, so you're waiting for me too, are you?"

She reached down and swung the cat up into her arms. As she did so, a voice drifted up from the platform where her little house sat. "Indie? Is that you?"

She accepted the inevitable. "Yes, Vi, it's me. I'll be there in a moment."

Violet Sherman was on her feet by the time Indigo reached her, her hands twisted into knots. Since the trees didn't encroach upon either of the old platforms, or the sunken garden between them, there was some light here from the full moon. It shimmered on the glass panels of her front wall and showed up the gauntness of her sister's features. Indigo was shocked. The normally well-put-together Violet Sherman was as rumpled and uncoordinated as a bag lady. The problem was obviously a major one.

"Where have you been?" Violet's voice was strained, as if her throat was constricted. "Maisie phoned hours ago to say you were on your way back."

"It takes two hours to get from London, and then I had to get away from Mr and Mrs Fielding." Indigo crossed to the door of her house and opened it, placing Midnight on the ground so she could go inside. Then she turned back to her sister. "What are you doing here, Vi? Surely this could have waited until daytime?"

"No, it couldn't." The voice began to shake and tears appeared in the reddened eyes, making Indigo feel guilty for her lack of sympathy. She noticed the other woman wasn't even wearing any makeup, which was unheard of.

"What is it then? Tell me."

"Alan's been arrested. He's on remand in Lewes."

Now that was a shock. Her timid, mild-mannered nephew wasn't the sort to get himself into trouble, not serious trouble. People only got put on remand for major offences. "Arrested? For what?"

"Murder."

The proverbial chill ran down her spine and her first thought was 'not again!' She stared at her sister. "Please say you're joking."

"Would I joke about that?" Violet spun, walked to the far end of the platform, turned again and came back. "He didn't do it, Indie. It's not like Paul, but that makes it even worse. Alan's an innocent. At least Paul had experience of criminals, and he still couldn't face spending time in prison. What am I going to do?"

Indigo reached out and flicked the switch inside her door, turning on a number of inner lights that spilled through the glass and illuminated the platform. "You'd better come in."

Once Violet was settled on the sofa, Indigo flopped down beside her and turned to face her. "Okay, tell me what's happened. How long has Alan been inside?"

"Two weeks."

"What! Why didn't you ask Maisie to let me know?"

There was a pathetic tone to her sister's voice when she answered. "I did, but she refused to pass the message on. We had quite a fight about it. Your partner can be pretty damned Aussie when she wants to be."

Indigo knew exactly what Violet meant. There were times when Maisie's antipodean background came very much to the fore, especially when she was leaping to the defence of someone she cared about. She'd mention it when she next saw her, but could guess why Maisie had refused Violet's request. "Sorry. She was probably trying to keep me focused on the task in hand."

"But Alan's your nephew. Surely that was more important?"

There was no answer to that. All she could do was study her sister's drawn features and the red-rimmed eyes. By the look of it, she'd had little sleep over the past two weeks and was on the verge of collapse. A knot started to form itself in her own stomach. She heard herself say, "Alan couldn't kill anyone. He gets upset if he accidently steps on an ant."

"Don't you think I know that!"

"Of course." She put her arm around the other's shoulders, feeling the shudder in her thin frame as she drew tortured breaths. "Who's he supposed to have killed? And why do the police think he did it?"

Violet was silent for a moment, gulping down air. When she'd calmed down enough to speak, her voice was low and tremulous. "It was a man called Peter Taylor. He was something to do with the road builders, I think. And, oh Indie, the police found Alan's medical bracelet beside the body. The one for his asthma."

For a moment, the information made no sense, then enlightenment dawned. She groaned. "He found the body, didn't he? And the first thing he did was run away and hide."

Her sister nodded, misery etched into every line of her face. "That's what he says. You know what he's like. But the police won't believe him. You should see what that horrible man has said about him to the Press. He's not describing my baby at all."

"Horrible man?"

"Some police inspector. Waters, I think he's called." She rubbed at her eyes, achieving nothing more than to redden them further.

Indigo reached out and placed her free hand on her sister's knee. "Vi, you're dead on your feet and I'm not much better. Go home, get some sleep, and come to the office at ten."

"But —"

"No buts. We're not going to solve anything in this state"

Reluctantly, Violet dragged herself to her feet and, ushered by Indigo, left the little house and started up the path towards the road. Indigo watched her go with some trepidation, wondering how safe it was for her sister to drive in that state. Luckily, there wouldn't be much traffic on the road at that time of the morning.

Her thoughts were interrupted by a soft head butting her leg. She looked down. "I know, Midnight, you want to be fed. Come to think of it, so do I." Closing the door, she made her way towards the tiny kitchen, closely followed by an anxious cat.

She'd meant to grab a shower and a quick bite to eat, then fall gratefully into her own bed for a well earned sleep, but Violet's news had disturbed her. She prepared cat food for Midnight and a sandwich for herself in a distracted manner, almost putting Sheba in her sandwich and tuna down for the cat. Correcting herself in time, she placed the bowl in front of a disappointed looking feline and took her sandwich across to her desk.

Within minutes, lurid headlines were screaming at her from her laptop. **'Protester kills Road Consultant!'**, **'19-year-old man arrested for axe murder!'**, **'Bypass consultant brutally murdered!'**. The gist of the story seemed to be that a consultant working for the company building the Great Oxing bypass had been found dead in Oxley Woods, his head caved in by a sharp instrument, thought to be a small axe. The more she read, the more convinced she was that her nephew Alan was psychologically incapable of the crime.

She stopped reading and sat back in her seat, thinking through the background to the case. Great Oxing was one of those medieval walled towns that had sprawled out well beyond the original centre. Enough of the walls and old street layout existed to make driving through the town a nightmare. Plans for a bypass road had been batted about the district council for years, but a route had recently been pushed through the planning committee and work had begun, with a company called Henckle and Green employed to build the road. However, the final route involved destroying a swathe of ancient woodland, which had brought the protesters out in force.

"My woodland," she said aloud, thinking that the road would be built not too far from her home, which had once been Oxley Woods railway station.

Alan had come to her to ask whether he should join the eco-protesters camped out in the wood, and she'd encouraged him to do so. She'd been as angry as he was about the proposed desecration of these old woods, but that wasn't the reason she'd told him to do it. He was due to go to university in September. That would have been next week, the start of the semester.

"I thought the experience might help him launch himself into university life. Get him used to mixing a bit better." There was a mew of enquiry from Midnight, who had paused in the middle of cleaning her belly. "Am I responsible for all this?" She asked the cat.

Midnight ignored her and went back to her postprandial cleaning. Indigo sighed and opened some of the articles, reading through various versions of what had happened. The victim, one Peter K. Taylor, had been employed as a consultant by Henckle and Green to help them negotiate with Oxley District Council. One paper said he was an ex senior planning officer with a South London council, giving him insight and bureaucratic skills when dealing with local government. He did not, however, appear to have much in the way of skills when it came to dealing with people. There had apparently been several run-ins with the protesters, the last happening just days before his death. The details caused her to shake her head in frustration. According to the reporter, during this encounter Alan Sherman had punched Taylor and knocked him to the floor.

"He wouldn't do that. Damn it, Alan's default position is to run away."

Midnight, tired of the one-sided conversation, stood up and made a dignified retreat into the bedroom. Indigo opened another article, and almost immediately came upon a name she knew – Inspector George Howard. Something in her chest tightened. Why did George have to be involved? She'd been looking forward to their reunion, but now it would be spoilt by his association with Alan's case.

She forced herself to read on. George had been the arresting officer, but it seemed Chief Inspector Richard Waters had been the SIO, and the man feeding all the information to the press. His description of her nephew as a callous and fanatical eco-warrior made a small vein throb in her temple. This was a man who had no doubts at all that they'd arrested the right person, yet there seemed no real evidence apart from the purported earlier attack.

She sat back again and dropped her head into her hands. It was a complete mess. Alan had been arrested, charged with murder, and remanded to Lewes Prison, just as Violet had said. Yet none of it made sense. Something had to be done, but what? She could guess what her sister wanted of her. No doubt she thought a Private Investigator could just go out and track down the real killer. But this was the UK, not some American noir thriller.

"We don't do murder cases."

Her voice sounded doubtful, even to herself. Violet had been right about one thing. They couldn't let Alan go the same way as his Uncle Paul. She yawned and realised she was probably too tired to think straight. There was one thing she could do in the morning before going into the office. She turned off the laptop and stood up. Midnight had had the right idea. It was time for bed.

"Indie! What are you doing here this early?"

He'd come to the door looking tousled and not quite awake, and the sight of him made her heart thump. The look suited him, much more than his serious and somewhat stuffy police persona. She took a deep breath. It was seven thirty, she hadn't been able to sleep any longer, and now two halves of her personal life were about to clash. "Why have you arrested Alan?"

"Alan?"

"Alan Sherman, my nephew."

His initial puzzlement turned to shock and he stood looking at her for a long moment. "Sherman's your nephew? I ... see."

There had been a subtle change in his tone and it worried her. "He's not guilty." It came out sharper than she'd intended and she tried to soften her voice as she continued. "George, you've got it all wrong. Alan is the quietest, most timid boy you could imagine. There's no way he could have killed that man."

"He's not a boy."

Now she understood. The tone was that of the policeman, not the lover. What was happening? Hadn't they grown close these past four months? Close enough to share and discuss problems, work out solutions. She swallowed. "If you've charged him on the basis of that dropped bracelet, you're making a bad mistake."

"I'm sorry, Miss Lattimer, I can't discuss the case with you. Enquiries are ongoing."

His tone and expression might have become official, but there was something in his eyes that suggested distress. She wanted to reach out, to ask him to lighten up, help her out, but she knew him well enough to know he would never compromise a case.

Before she could think of a suitable response, he frowned and ran his fingers through his thick grey hair, disturbing it even more than it had been. "This is bad. I can't be in a relationship with the aunt of the accused. I'm sorry, Indie. The past months have been fun, but this has to be the end. From now on it looks like we're on different sides."

A gasp was wrung from her depths. "George—"

But he'd stepped back and closed the door, shutting her out. Stunned, she stood unmoving for a few minutes, her pulse racing. That wasn't at all the way the visit was meant to go. Damn the man! She hadn't reached the age of thirty-four without having a couple of brief relationships, but she'd never been in love before. Not like this. Not totally and completely smitten. Now he was willing to throw it all away, just so he could continue to persecute an innocent boy. And Alan was a boy, no matter what he said.

"But he doesn't love me." The realisation came unbidden and left a sick feeling in her gut. He'd never said the 'L' word, and he'd always been just that little bit removed, as if ready to back away at a moment's notice. She gave a grim laugh. Wasn't that what he'd just done?

So, what had she expected? Maybe her intentions hadn't been quite as clear as they might have been. Somehow she'd hoped George would solve the problem, back off, tell her they had other suspects. But her knight hadn't ridden to the rescue and she was on her own. Where did she go from here? Back to the office. Back to talk with her staff and her sister. There must be some way forward.

She turned and walked away from the unwelcoming door.

Chapter Two

Maisie Mitchell was seated in her usual position behind the reception desk, but it was obvious she'd been waiting for Indigo and not concentrating on her work. She jumped up as soon as the latter closed the agency door behind her and came to block her path. "Your sister's waiting in your office."

Indigo glanced at the clock. It was nine twenty-five. "She's early. I told her to be here at ten."

"You can't blame her." The red-head grimaced. "Look, about her message —"

She waved the explanation away. "You didn't want me to have to choose between Chloe and Alan. I know how your mind works." She studied her friend and partner thoughtfully. "But it was my decision to make."

"It was a bugger of a choice, pet, so I made it for you."

There was that maternal protection coming to the fore again. Indigo heaved a deep sigh. There was no way she'd win this argument. Best to let the matter drop. "She told you the situation?"

Maisie nodded and returned to her chair, her naturally cheerful face clouded by concern. "It's a bloody mess, ain't it? I'd be chewing bricks if it was one of my boys." Her eyes strayed to a photo of her family that occupied pride of place on the corner of her desk.

"I'm pretty sure he didn't do it. Alan's not that kind of boy."

"Not a boy any more," Maisie said, echoing George. "But you're right. I reckon that young bloke's too squeamish to kill someone. I'd like my boys to grow up that polite."

Indigo nodded and made for her office. The room was as warm and comforting as it had always been. The soft, crumpled brown leather chair that fitted itself to her form; the polished oak desk with its red leather inlay; the lacquer cabinet, its Japanese figures picked out in gold. This was the haven that normally welcomed her back from her trawls through littered big city back streets, but today it failed to lift her spirits, largely due to the sad figure standing with her back to the door. Violet was looking out of the window onto the bustling city scene below, but her posture suggested she wasn't seeing the view before her.

"Vi?"

Her sister turned, and she was relieved to see the make-up, the pressed clothes and the slight easing of tension. But the eyes still held pain and the voice was dull and weary. "Sorry I'm early."

"That's okay. Sit down."

A few minutes later, with Indigo in her own chair and Violet perched on the edge of the visitor chair, her hands gripped too tightly around her handbag, Indigo tried to break the tension. "This isn't going to go the same way as Paul."

"You can't say that. Paul had been around. He did drugs. He dealt with criminals. But he killed himself rather than face a life sentence. What do you think that would do to Alan? God knows what's happening to him already."

The voice was edged with the toxin of despair and Indigo decided to come straight out with her decision. "Look, Vi, I can look at what evidence they've got and try to refute it. I've been thinking about it. If Alan's innocent then their evidence must have weaknesses. But I do need access to that evidence and George refused to tell me anything."

"If he's innocent?" Then her brows puckered. "Who's George?"

It was a shock to realise she'd never introduced her lover to her family. Not even mentioned him to anyone but Maisie. Come to think of it, she hadn't met his daughters either. Had they been so wrapped up in each other? "A friend of mine," she muttered.

Violet wasn't listening, being occupied with scrabbling through her handbag. Eventually, she brought out a small white card which she handed over. "I've been on the phone to our solicitor. I told him about you and what you do, and asked him if it would be okay for you to look into things. He says the defence is allowed to make its own enquiries, but you'd get on better if you were part of the team."

She took the card and studied it. It was elegant and discreet. The name Tony Dawson of Dawson, Purvis and Aitchison, was printed in raised silver letters on good quality white card. It looked expensive, not the card of a solicitor who was used to being roused from his bed in the wee hours to defend a small-time burglar. It was a good job her brother-in-law was well paid.

"You will contact him, won't you?"

She gave her sister a reassuring smile. "Yes, Vi, I'll contact him. But I won't be constrained by him, so I hope he's not that type. I need a free hand to do things my own way."

That brought a tiny, sad flash of a smile. "Haven't you always?" She swallowed and appeared to be fighting back tears. "It will be alright, won't it?"

Indigo rose, came round the desk, and enveloped her sister in a hug. "If there is any evidence out there to exonerate Alan, I'll find it. I promise."

Violet collapsed against her chest and the tears won the fight. "Thank you, Indie. I've been so worried. Matt's striding around the house hitting things, and the girls are hiding in their rooms. This past two weeks have been a nightmare."

Indigo held her and rocked her until the tears subsided and Violet struggled to be free. Once released, she groped in her bag for a handkerchief and rubbed vigorously at her face, smudging her eye make up into a bruise-like mess. She then stuffed the dirty handkerchief back into her bag and got unsteadily to her feet. "You will let me know how things are going, won't you?"

"I'll give you regular updates. Now go home and calm down."

Indigo walked to the door and held it open, then escorted her sister out of the room and through the reception area. Having watched her descend unsteadily down towards ground level, she turned to find a pair of hazel eyes watching her warily.

"What are you going to do?"

"Try to find out what really happened." She pulled a visitor chair over from the waiting area and sat facing Maisie across her desk.

"Are you sure you want to know that, pet? I've been thinking. What if young Alan acted totally out of character and bashed the bloke? It happens, you know, on the spur of the moment."

Did she want to know? Yes, she'd already faced all the possibilities. She nodded. "Whichever way it goes, Maisie. It's not like I haven't been down this route before."

"Your brother?"

"Paul, yes. But they're two totally different personalities. I'm as sure as I can be that Alan is incapable of caving a man's head in with an axe." An unexpected laugh escaped her. "Damn it. He'd have dropped the weapon at the first sight of blood. I hate to say it, but my nephew's a bit of a wimp. His sisters used to have to stand up to the bullies on his behalf."

Maisie chuckled along with her. "What can I do to help then?"

She stood up and handed over the white and silver business card. "Make me an appointment with Alan's solicitor, will you? As soon as possible, please. Alan's been inside two weeks already."

Tony Dawson's offices were as elegant and discreet as his card had been, being situated in what had once been a three story townhouse in a quiet avenue of Nunsfield. He was one of three partners in the business, all of whom had their offices on the first floor, with the ground floor reserved for reception and clerical activities. As she entered the seriously understated room with its deep pile, dark blue carpet, Dawson rose to greet her and shake her hand. He was in his late thirties at a guess, wearing a smart, dark grey suit and subdued yellow tie. He gave a quick professional smile that didn't touch his eyes and waved her towards a chair placed directly in front of his oversized desk.

"Mrs Sherman told me you might be joining the defence team," he said once she was seated.

Joining the defence team. It sounded very professional, but rather stuffy. She could already feel rules and regulations constricting around her, causing tension in her shoulders. She met the clear grey eyes on the other side of the desk. "Let's be frank from the start. I've never done criminal work before, but I seem to have a knack for getting information out of people."

"A useful skill," he murmured, then paused and gave her what could only be described as a searching look. "I'm glad we're being frank, Miss Lattimer, because I'm not sure how much use you're going to be to us."

That made her eyebrows rise. "Then why did you agree to meet me?"

"Your sister wants you involved and she's paying the bills."

What a brazen statement. How could he sit there and say that without embarrassment? "Well, that is frank. If you don't feel the need for an investigator, perhaps I should continue as an independent."

"No, no." He waved a hand at her. "Look, I have worked with private investigators in the past. It's just that, as you said yourself, this is outside your area of expertise."

She leant forward, deliberately encroaching into his space. "Vi asked me to find evidence to help Alan's case. I'm perfectly capable of doing that. I may specialise in finding runaway teenagers, but I take other cases as well, and my staff have their own skills and experience."

He put his hands together, fingertip to fingertip and sat studying her for a while. Then he nodded and sat upright. "Okay we'll go ahead, but please remember you're part of the team. Anything illegal will reflect on this partnership and we can't have that."

"I don't do illegal," she said stiffly. "Just what kind of investigator do you think I am?"

He ignored the indignant comment, saying, "Now, let's get down to the evidence, shall we."

Still fuming, she fought an urge to get up and walk out, knowing her relationship to Alan made that impossible. Why on earth had Matt and Vi hired this insufferable man? He'd have to be an exceptional solicitor to be worth putting up with this kind of insulting behaviour. Although something told her his attitude towards his employers was probably very different.

Appearing to not even notice he'd insulted her, Dawson launched into a discussion of the evidence."You know about the bracelet, of course. Apparently it had a faulty catch. The police have verified that."

"I know about the bracelet," she said through clenched teeth, "and there was talk in the press about some vomit."

Dawson pulled a face at the word. "The DNA evidence, yes." He tapped his finger absently against his desk. "I'm afraid there's more. Crumpled at the back of Alan's tent was a t-shirt which was covered with spots of the victim's blood. It also has a small patch of material torn out of it. That fabric, attached to a 'Save the Trees' badge, was found on the floor of Taylor's car."

Not just evidence of Alan finding the body then? She seized on the latter sentence. "Tell me about the car. According to the internet it was found in the Aldgate car park."

"It seems to have been left there by the killer. The police believe it was first used to transport Taylor's body to the woods."

"Are you saying the woodland path was a dump site?"

His eyes narrowed and she had the impression he was watching to see what she'd make of the information. "Apparently so. There's evidence the body was briefly wrapped in plastic. The police case is that Alan's bracelet fell off while he was wrapping the body and dropped onto Taylor's chest when he rolled him under the bush."

"That makes no sense," she said, and saw a glimmer of approval enter his eyes. "Why would Alan dump the body near his camp? If he was going to move it, he'd take it somewhere far away."

His face broke into a full, honest smile for the first time since they'd met. "Bravo, Miss Lattimer. That's one weakness we can attack in the prosecution case. It is, of course, irrational for a killer to murder someone and then deliberately leave the body on their own doorstep."

The smile lessened her antipathy a little. Maybe he was on their side after all. "You think Alan's innocent, don't you?"

"I do. It's not necessary, of course, for a solicitor to believe in the innocence of his client, but that young nephew of yours strikes me as a very unlikely killer." He reached up to scratch the side of his face, giving an exaggerated sigh. "Unfortunately, there's a lot stacked against him. If you can untangle even a quarter of it, I'd be grateful. This is one hell of a case to defend."

"You'd better tell me the worst."

"Let's start with the car. The killer was seen driving it into the car park. A witness describes a young man with fair hair. She failed to pick Alan out of a line up, which is good for us, and we can make some play on her age, since she's eighty six. But, to be honest, she's no daffy old dear and her description of the man she saw does fit Alan. To make matters worse, the car seat had been adjusted to suit someone of his height."

"Adjusted?"

"Taylor was a tall man, six foot two. The driver's seat had been pulled forwards. The police forensics people estimate the killer to be around five foot eleven."

Exactly Alan's height. For an innocent youth, he certainly seemed to be having a streak of bad luck. She sought around for something to exonerate him. "I don't see Alan driving a car by himself," she said eventually. "He doesn't have a full licence, and he gave up learning after his fifth lesson because the traffic made him nervous."

"I'm afraid that won't help us. The prosecution would simply argue he did it because he had to. Five lessons are enough to learn how to operate a car."

"What about the murder weapon? Surely there must be fingerprints or something?"

"It hasn't been found, but they believe it was a small hand axe." He met her eyes and she was surprised to see sympathy in his. "They had one at the camp which they used to chop firewood. Unfortunately, it's gone missing, so the police couldn't check it for blood. In it's absence they've quite naturally assumed it to be the murder weapon. I'm sorry. I did say it was a hell of a case."

She groaned and buried her head in her hands. No wonder he'd said she wouldn't be able to help. The evidence might be circumstantial, but it was all stacked against her nephew. Was there any light in the darkness? She sat up, working it through in her mind. Maybe there was a way in. What if she took each piece of evidence in turn and tried to unravel it? She turned to Dawson. "Can I get in to see Alan?"

"You could get a visit as a relative, but I think it would be better if you went in as part of the defence team. He's on remand, which means he's allowed unlimited visits from his legal representative. I do have to give forty eight hours notice, though, so it won't be tomorrow. Is there anything else you want?"

"I could do with a copy of the evidence. I need to study it to decide on my first move."

"We only have what the police have released to us. It doesn't include witness statements, I'm afraid, just a précis of what was said. It's early days yet, they'll have to give us more later. I can get my secretary to write a copy of our file to a USB stick for you. As part of the team you can see anything I'm privy to. Just don't go leaving it open to public view."

She started to protest, then thought better of it. She was just going to have to learn to ride the insults. "Thank you," she said meekly.

"I'll let the police know you've joined us, of course. We don't want them thinking you're a reporter, do we?"

It was meant as a joke and she granted him a forced laugh. This was testing her patience. Something about the untouched appearance of the office, and the stiff formality of the man, was stirring bad memories from her childhood. She got to her feet with a decisive nod. "You'll let me know about seeing Alan?"

He looked startled at her abrupt move but also rose, coming round the desk to shake her hand. As he opened the door, he said, "I'll have my secretary arrange things with the prison. She'll let you know when we can go in."

"Perhaps she could liaise with my personal assistant," she replied, determined not to be pushed into a subordinate role.

His lips twitched, causing her to wonder if there was a human being inside that sober suit after all. "Of course," he murmured. “If you’ll stop by her office on the way out, I’ll call down and ask her to give you that stick.”

As it happened, Dawson’s secretary proved scarily efficient. She had the USB stick ready and labelled before Indigo even found her office, and the interview with Alan had been arranged and communicated to Maisie by the time she got back to the agency.

Chapter Three

Lattimer Investigations occupied a self-contained suite of offices above a dentist, just off the main shopping street in Great Oxing. Two flights of grey-carpeted stairs led up to the offices from a plain blue door, which sat anonymously between the clinical frontage of the dental practice and the enticing photographic display of an Estate Agent. Only a small metal plaque on the door itself told potential clients the agency was there. There was no parking on the street in front, but an alley at the back provided delivery facilities to the shops and a few cramped parking spaces for their staff. It was a nuisance, since there was no back entrance to the agency, but Indigo kidded herself the walk gave her valuable exercise.

Today she took the stairs two at a time and disappeared into her office to review the evidence. In some strange way, Dawson's doubts about her ability had acted as a challenge and she was eager to see what holes she could poke in the police case. She set her laptop on the desk and started wading through the evidence. Only the tamest crime scene photos had been included, but there were reports from both the pathologist and the forensics laboratory, though she was aware these would have been checked and edited. Luckily, there was little the police could legitimately keep from the defence.

There was also the précis of the witness statements, mostly from the protestors and mostly of limited value. The statement that caught her attention was one from the elderly woman who'd seen Taylor's car being driven into the Aldgate car park. The police had kept back her name, but an internet check of the news coverage revealed it to be Mrs Hunter, an 86-year-old widow of Weymouth Avenue, Great Oxing. So much for the police protecting witnesses, with a free press and an even freer internet to spill the beans.

She read and reread the evidence, looking for weaknesses, and was doing a final check when her desk phone rang and she reached for it without taking her eyes from the screen. "Lattimer Investigations. Indigo Lattimer speaking."

"What the hell are you doing getting involved in my murder case? When I said we'd be on opposite sides, I didn't mean literally."

The voice on the other end of the phone was so unexpected that her grip on the receiver weakened and she only just managed to retrieve it before it crashed onto her desk. "George?"

"Yes." There was a short pause and she got the impression he was struggling to stay calm and polite. "Sorry, I thought Maisie had announced me."

"No."

"I didn't mean to shout at you." Another pause, and she could imagine him running his fingers through his hair, a habit he had when he was disturbed. "Look, Indie, you don't have the skills for this. Just leave it to the police."

"The police seem determined to railroad my nephew."

There was a gasp. "Damn it, that's unfair. We're just following the evidence."

"A limited set of evidence. It seems to me there's a vast range of people you haven't even bothered to talk to."

He immediately went on the defensive. "There was an obvious suspect. We can't waste taxpayers money by getting into irrelevant details."

It sounded so much as if he was quoting someone else that it made her think. Was it DCI Waters who had gone for the easy route? "You don't seem happy about that."

"It's not up to me to second guess the SIO."

And yet —. She knew George, knew what a stickler he was for the truth. Maybe he was being forced down a path he didn't want to follow. Had he overreacted to the news of her relationship to Alan because he was feeling unsure of his case? Or was he hoping his current enquiries would prove whether Alan was actually guilty or not?

"Indie? Are you going to back off?"

"No, of course I'm not. But here's an offer. If I find out anything I think you need to know, I'll contact you."

"Gee, thanks."

"Don't be like that." Damn! Damn! Damn! She hated this sudden estrangement, and she hated his apparent willingness to break up, as if he had no feelings for her at all.

Yet his next words were almost tender. "Be careful, sweetheart."

She was about to ask if that meant he thought the killer was still out there, but he'd put the phone down. She replaced her own receiver and sat looking at it for a long moment. What was going on between them? Did he care, or didn't he? She gave a growl of frustration, then jumped to her feet and strode into the outer office.

Maisie raised her arms into a mock defensive position. "Don't get cranky. I thought you'd appreciate a call from lover boy."

"George and I have split up."

"No! How'd that happen?"

Indigo felt herself droop, as if her muscle fibres had suddenly snapped. "To tell you the truth, I'm not sure. I went to see him early this morning."

"About the case?"

"About Alan. He said he couldn't continue to be in a relationship with me because I was related to his suspect. Then he slammed the door in my face."

"Oh." Maisie studied her silently. "Well, it'll work itself out. What you need is some lunch. It's past three. I'll just pop into the kitchen and rustle up a sandwich."

Indigo shook her head and returned to her office. Maisie, the Earth Mother, who thought everything could be solved with food and a cup of tea.

If Indigo had been shocked by her sister's appearance, she was stunned by the way her nephew looked. Fine-boned like his mother, his usual appearance was that of a much younger boy, all fresh-faced and hopeful. Now he'd shrunk into a little old man through stress, his skin dull and lined, his eyes wary. Having herself found the grey walls of the Victorian prison intimidating as they closed around her, she could understand how awful it must be for a timid boy from a middle class home. She stepped forward, raising her arms to give him a hug, but Dawson caught her shoulder and shook his head.

Instead, they sat at the table, Dawson and herself across from Alan, who struggled to produce a weak smile. "Hello, Aunt Indie."

She leant forward slightly. "It's okay, Alan, we're going to fix this. I just need a little time, and I need you to tell me everything that happened."

For a moment she thought he was going to burst into tears. "I don't know what happened. I just found it there, why won't anyone believe me?"

Having read the pathologist's report on the body, Indigo knew why her nephew referred to the dead man as 'it', and why he'd been sick. Taylor's head had been pulped so badly it was unrecognisable as human. She nodded reassurance. "We do believe you, but you know more than you think you do." He was going to protest, so she raised a hand. "It's true, Alan, people don't always recognise useful information. That's my job. Now, let's start with why you joined the protest group."

The blue eyes blinked at her in puzzlement. "You know, Aunt Indie. You encouraged me."

That was something she didn't need reminding of, she was already feeling guilty enough on that score. "Okay, let me tell you. When you heard about the change of route and the damage it would do to Oxley Woods, you were upset. You'd roamed those woods with me as a child and couldn't bear to think of all the plants and animals being killed. With the long holiday between school and university coming up, you heard about the protest camp and decided to join them. Is that about right?"

He nodded, saw Tony Dawson's eyes on him and blushed. "I thought we'd stand in front of bulldozers or something, but the road hasn't got that far yet. It was all rather uncomfortable, and a bit boring."

"Until you found the body." He flinched and she wished there was some kinder way of interrogating him, but there wasn't. "We have to talk about it," she said. "Tell me what happened."

He moved his mouth, but no sound came out. Then his tongue flickered back and forth across his lips allowing him to find his voice. "I was coming back from ... from walking in the woods and I saw this foot sticking out of a bush. I thought it was a stupid prank, a false leg or something." He took another couple of nervous licks at his mouth. "The guys were always doing things to spook Amy."

She'd never seen him so miserable, not even when he'd come off his bike and broken his shin bone. She tried to sound encouraging. "Go on."

"It was dreadful, really dreadful. You can't imagine."

"I can imagine," she said quietly, "I've read the reports."

His facial muscles flickered into the semblance of a smile. "You must think I'm a bit of a baby, Aunt Indie. Mum says you go to all sorts of horrible places, but it was a big fright for me. I wish I'd never pulled those branches back."

"That's when your bracelet came off?"

"I guess so. It was loose. It must have fallen off when I let go of the branches. They snapped back and scratched my hand."

"Then you were sick on the path and ran back to camp. Why didn't you tell anyone what you'd seen?"

The blue eyes widened in terror. "I couldn't do that. I mean, I didn't even want to think about it. I lay down in my tent and closed my eyes and tried to pretend it wasn't real. I wanted to go home to Mum."

Indigo gave a gasp of dismay. "Thank God you didn't, that would really have sealed your guilt in the eyes of the law." She frowned at him, considering her next question. "Alright, what about the t-shirt? Were you wearing it that day?"

He gave a frantic shake of his head. "I kept telling them I wasn't wearing it. It got dirty and torn a few days before. I just threw it in a corner. I thought Mum could mend it."

"How did it get torn?" She knew the answer from her internet trawl of newspaper articles but wanted the story in his own words.

It was as if she'd given him permission to relax by turning the talk down safer paths. He sat back, gave a small sigh and frowned in concentration, visualising a memory. "We were walking through the woods —"

"We?"

"Me, Mike Nash and Amy. We'd been gathering firewood. We used the fire for cooking and stuff." The shudder he gave told her exactly what he thought of the privations of camping and made her smile. "Well, we were walking through the woods and we came across two men in suits. They were standing on the path ahead of us, taking measurements or something. It was Amy who started everything. She takes dope, so she gets a bit weird sometimes."

He appeared to consider the weirdness of drug addicts for a moment, then shook his head and continued. "She started screaming at them about killing things. She was worried about her fairies."

"Fairies?"

He met her eyes and gave an embarrassed little laugh. "Amy thinks there are fairies living near the pond and she says the plants talk to her. She got very angry with the men and the younger one looked really scared. I guess Amy can be frightening, what with the green hair and all, and Mike's tough looking. He frightens me sometimes, especially when he's been drinking."

"Taylor didn't appear to be afraid?"

"Who?"

"The older man." Did he actually understand who the body in the woods belonged to?

"Oh no. He was annoyed, if anything. He said we were trespassing, which we weren't. It's a public space, people walk there all the time."

"How did he get knocked down," she prompted, steering him back on course.

"Well, as I said, Amy set things off by shouting. Then the older man, Mr Taylor, said something about trees being an inefficient use of space and that riled Mike, of course. I mean he's an animal rights activist, so it was bound to. Especially when Mr Taylor said he didn't care how many spotted toads died as long as he could improve traffic flow around Great Oxing. That was a red rag to Mike. He said Mr Taylor should be strung —" Realising what he was saying he came to an abrupt halt. "He didn't mean it, of course. None of us actually wanted to hurt anyone."

So, thought Indigo, it looks like Mike Nash is worth looking into. Why didn't the police at least check him out? Could DCI Waters have been even more blinkered than she was beginning to think? Perhaps the press stories about Alan hitting Taylor were also inaccurate. Perhaps it was Nash who'd struck out. She asked the question again. "But Mr Taylor did get hurt, didn't he? Who punched him?"

"Nobody hit him, not on purpose. I told you, we'd been collecting firewood. Amy was throwing her arms about and she was holding this tree branch. Mr Taylor stepped too close to her and I could see he was going to get hit, so I tried to move him away and ... well, I tripped and bumped into him. He grabbed at me and we both fell on the floor. I don't know how he cut himself. His hand was bleeding, maybe the branch caught him. I didn't notice the tear in my shirt until later, and I don't know how my badge got in his car."

Indigo sat and pondered. She could just see Alan diffidently trying to protect Taylor and succeeding only in knocking him over. His instincts were good, but they clashed with his dislike of putting himself forward, and that sometimes made him clumsy. But then she knew and understood the boy, she wasn't sure how well his explanation would go down in court. Especially if he hesitated when describing how he found the body, like he had with her. She knew a secret when she came across one, and her nephew was hiding something. Which was also extremely unlike him.

The room had become incredibly quiet and she looked up to find two sets of male eyes watching her intently. She gave them what she hoped was a reassuring smile. "There are things I can work with. That t-shirt for one. Somebody must have noticed what you were wearing the day Taylor was killed."

Alan looked downcast at the thought. "Not Amy, she was really out of it that day. She'd got hold of some strong stuff from somewhere and I saw her floating around in the woods like she was on another planet. I said to ... I told someone she looked like Peter Pan."

There was that hesitation again, and another suspect. Maybe Amy got high and beat Taylor to a pulp for killing her fairies? Indigo gave herself a mental shake. Forget Peter Pan, this case was starting to sound like Alice in Wonderland. She rose to her feet and turned to Dawson. "I think I've learnt all I can here. It's time for me to start looking for evidence."

They said goodbye to Alan and started on their way through the cold, uncarpeted corridors towards the exit, their feet echoing like the Victorian ghosts she thought must haunt this daunting place. After a few minutes Dawson suddenly said, "Where do you plan to start?"

She glanced sideways at him in surprise. "The woods, of course, assuming the protest camp is still there. That's where the body was found and where the police think the motive lies. I'm not convinced about the latter, but it's as good a starting point as any."

He nodded his approval of her decision. "You'll keep me fully informed, of course."

Her eyes veiled. She didn't like this attempt of his to direct her enquiries. She was her own woman and used to running things her way. "I'll keep my sister fully informed," she said calmly. "I'll let you know of anything relevant to your case."

He didn't comment, but she thought she saw a slight smile cross his features.

Chapter Four

As she drove out of town towards Oxley Woods, Indigo felt less and less confident of her ability to get a handle on the murder. She'd reread the police files after getting back from the prison and there really didn't seem to be any other obvious suspect than Alan. Mike Nash and Amy Dwyer were her two best leads. They'd been the other two people involved in the clash between Taylor and the protestors, but the motivation for them was as weak as it was for her nephew.

She passed slowly through the narrow opening of Aldgate in a line of crawling cars. The chunks of original medieval wall made the city very attractive, especially to tourists, but it was hell to drive through. The bypass was long overdue. How many years had it been stalled by various interest groups who didn't want it going this way or that? Five or six since the initial council decision to relieve the congestion.

Turning left off the main A road she came into a narrow country lane which ran alongside this section of woods and slowed slightly as she tried to spot the best place to park for the protestors' camp. For a few minutes there was open heathland on her right hand side and woodland to her left. Then the heath gave way to a barrier of trees, through which she caught the odd glimpse of closely mown grass. She passed a sign that read 'Great Oxing Golf and Country Club' and nodded to herself. The camp should be somewhere around here.

The next question was where to park. If she left the car at the roadside it would be a hazard, since there was barely enough room for two cars to pass each other along this stretch. There was a small lay-by further along the road, but that was quite a way from where she wanted to be. The only alternative was to pull over onto the verge. She drew to a halt and thought about it. The area between the road and the beginning of the tree line was a morass of weeds and scrub tall enough for her to be reluctant about exposing the underside of her car to it. Still, there was no other option. Accepting the inevitable with a sigh, she put the car into gear and edged carefully onto the verge, leaving only the offside tires on the road.

She'd worn her habitual jeans and soft leather boots for the trip into the woods, and was glad she'd done so as she pushed through unyielding greenery looking for a footpath. She knew there was one leading to the small clearing where the protest group had pitched its tents, but trees and bushes constantly thwarted her progress and forced her into so many twists and turns that she lost all sense of direction, until she even became unsure of the way back to the road. Just as she thought she'd become hopelessly lost, she stumbled onto the area containing the campsite and her first glance made her heart sink. There had been twenty six people in the group when the police interviewed them just after the murder. Now there were only three tents here, looking lost and pathetic amidst the dark, overhanging trees. No doubt most of the protestors had faded back to the various towns from which they'd come, not wanting to be associated with murder. She hoped fervently she wasn't going to need to track them all down.

She was standing at the edge of the camp, wondering where to start, when a man appeared out of the trees on the far side of the tents. She guessed he was in his thirties, though the scraggy, slightly greying beard made him look older. His hair was long and equally unkempt. His clothes were rumpled and mud spattered, but reasonably good underneath, like a slightly better class of tramp. The overall appearance was dark and heavy, apart from pale eyes that scowled at her under heavy brows.

"Go away," he said. "No visitors."

The accent was northern, possibly Yorkshire, but had been softened by education and travel. From the police notes she guessed this was the protestor's leader, a man with a history of student radicalism and animal rights activism.

She decided to start with an innocent smile, bearing in mind Alan's comments about him. "Mr Nash?"

"What if I am? Who's asking?"

She moved into conversation range. "My name's Indigo Lattimer," she said, holding out her hand. "I'm a private investigator. I've been hired to help Alan Sherman's defence team find evidence to help him."

He looked down at the hand, ignored it, half turned, and walked across to the embers of a camp fire. The area around the fire showed signs of being where the residents sat when they weren't in their tents. Nash dropped onto a flattened patch of grass and sat staring at the cold ashes with his legs crossed at the ankles. She followed him and sat down close by.

"I'd like to talk to you about Alan, and about Peter Taylor and what happened here." She pulled her phone from her pocket and displayed it. "Do you mind if I record our conversation?"

He growled at her. "You can talk all you want, I might even answer, but I'll not have you tape me so you can rearrange what I say and make me look guilty of summat."

She shrugged and put the phone on the ground beside her. The voice memos app was already open, so it was easy to set it working. As far as possible she recorded all her interviews. Sometimes she asked permission, often not. People were used to seeing phones around, and she'd become expert at switching the app on and off without being obvious. She'd asked Nash's permission merely to see how he'd react and was not disappointed.

"Alan Sherman was with your group for a few weeks," she began. "What did you think of him?"

"Middle class mummy's boy," he grunted. "Too damn polite for his own good. Just playing at saving the planet. What's his kind care about owt? They'll just buy their way out of trouble, when it comes." He glanced sideways at her. "You don't think a working class family could afford to hire a private investigator to save their little boy?" He sneered the words 'private investigator'.

Okay, thought Indigo, I know your type. Life has disappointed you, you hate anyone more successful, and you plan to take it out on every establishment figure that comes your way. She decided to let him lead the conversation and see where it took them.

"If he was such a wimp, surely he wasn't capable of beating Taylor's head to a pulp?"

"Didn't say he was. Police fitted him up. Surprised they didn't try pinning it on me, but then I'm not stupid enough to drop my ID on top of a corpse. For God's sake!"

"But Alan threatened Taylor, didn't he? A few days before the murder?"

He gave her another glance, his eyes shrewd and calculating. "No, he didn't, I did. Bastard deserved what he got. He actually said the world would be a better place if it was covered with concrete."

For a moment the cynical mask slipped and she saw real astonishment. It surprised her. Perhaps her initial assessment had been too glib. Maybe he did have some concern for nature, after all. He'd evidently found Peter Taylor's viewpoint to be totally alien to him.

"Can you tell me what happened when you and Alan met Taylor in the woods?"

"Not much to tell. Taylor was out there with a lackey, measuring up for the bulldozers. Crazy Amy was with us and she went postal. Started shouting, flinging her arms around, practically foaming at the mouth. Girl's paranoid, but what do you expect from a druggie?"

"How did Taylor react?"

"Told you. Said everyone would be better off in nice clean, efficient towns." Nash snorted and exaggerated his accent for effect. "Can't ever have visited t' North, or he'd know how dirty and inefficient towns can be. Industry's a bugger for dirt." He dropped back to a more neutral accent. "Only we don't have any industry any more, do we?"

She ignored the comment as an irrelevance. "So what caused you to threaten him?"

"Said it didn't matter a great deal if a few animals died to build his precious bypass. The bypass was of greater benefit to Oxley than a lot of vermin-ridden wildlife. Greater benefit, my foot! One day soon we'll run out of oil. What good will their efficient roads do them then? Hey?"

"That's when you hit him?"

Nash laughed out loud at this. "I didn't hit him, no one did. Got in the way of Crazy Amy. Told you she was flailing her arms about, with a branch in one hand. That idiot Sherman tried to stop him getting hit and knocked him on his arse. Laughed myself sick. Stupid man, sitting in the dirt, blood streaming down his nose, threatening to call the police down on us. Like we cared. We're protestors. Police are part of the package."

"You say his nose was bleeding? Alan says he cut his hand."

He shook his head with conviction. "Boy's confused. Amy caught him across the face with that stick she was holding. His nose bled. Must have put his hand up to try to stop the bleeding. Boy's right about one thing, he did have blood on his hand."

"But how did that blood get on Alan's t-shirt?"

"Good little boy helped him up, didn't he? All sorry and apologetic." Nash spat a casual swear word. "Should have left him down there. Only drew the stupid man's attention to himself."

She changed tack. "You had a small axe in the camp, didn't you? For cutting firewood?"

"Oh, the murder weapon? Police made a big thing out of that. Searched the entire campsite, including the loos. That was fun."

"But they didn't find it?"

"Course they didn't. Amy was the last person seen with it. Probably wandered off and gave it to those damn fairies of hers."

"Fairies?"

He motioned towards the depths of the woods. "There's a pond back there a way. Amy's convinced she sees fairies flying over it. Don't know where she gets her weed but it's pretty potent stuff. Keep telling her they're only dragonflies. Told the police Amy probably lost it back there. They dragged the pond, but it didn't turn up."

"Yes, I know the pond." She nodded, deciding she'd got all she could from Nash. There was only one question left to ask. "Alan says he came running back to camp after he found the body. Were you here that morning?"

"Do I have an alibi?" He laughed again. "Probably not. Was passed out in my tent, sleeping off a skinful from the night before."

"You were out drinking the night before the murder?"

"Now you're starting to sound like the cops. Was drinking from midday till they threw me out closing time. Didn't get back to camp till the wee hours. Bus stops running at seven, so I had to walk. Was so drunk I could barely stand up, but I managed it somehow. Have the instincts of a homing pigeon, me. Collapsed on top of my sleeping bag and didn't wake up till the cops dragged me out."

"What pub?"

He grinned, though there was no humour in it. "Waterman's Arms. Can't recommend it, they barred me. As I recall, I started ranting about the construction company and threatened to string 'em all up in the trees."

"You did?" She was surprised he would say something so incriminating.

He gave a casual shrug to indicate his lack of concern. "Just so you know, wasn't me drove Taylor's car, because I can't drive. Don't believe in private cars. Worst things ever invented." He paused, thought for a moment and amended, "one of the worst."

She didn't know how much trust she could place in that declaration. Nash might not have a licence, but it didn't mean he'd never learnt to drive a car. Maybe when he was young, before he got into ecology. She stood up and asked, "Is Amy still around?"

"She's still here. Just her and Abiola now. She'll be by the pond, I don't doubt."

She found Amy Dwyer exactly where Nash had said, sitting motionless, staring at the little patch of water. The pond was almost too small to be graced with that name, with two straight sides and one curved, like a slice of pie. The trees around it were sparser than elsewhere in the woods, allowing sunlight to filter through and reflect from the glassy surface. The curved edge was formed by a grassy bank, where Amy was sitting, knees raised and arms clasped round her shins. She looked up as Indigo approached.

"The fairies have all gone now."

Indigo studied her, trying to fit all she'd heard to the reality before her. The girl had an attractive face, heart-shaped and rather pixyish, with fine brows, wide eyes and a generous mouth. The effect was enhanced by the cap of apple green hair and the gold stud beneath her lower lip. She was dressed in a collection of bright pinks. As far as Indigo could tell from her vantage point, these consisted of a long skirt with a shorter one over the top, and a tunic over that. The clothes hung loosely on her skinny frame, but her eyes were relatively clear, so it seemed she wasn't stoned at the moment. Indigo dropped to the grass beside her.

"That's a shame," she said.

Amy turned towards her and gave a beaming smile. "I knew you'd understand. I like your hair. I tried mine blonde once, but it didn't suit me."

"Thank you." She took a deep breath and plunged in, tapping her phone back to record before speaking. "Amy, my name's Indie. I'm trying to help Alan Sherman. Would you answer some questions for me?"

"Oh, sure, I like Alan. I understand him killing that horrible man, but I'm sorry they're going to punish him for it."

"I'm not sure Alan did kill him. I'm trying to find out who did so we can get Alan out of jail."

Amy shook her head. "If Alan didn't kill him, maybe it was one of the monsters."

"Monsters?" Indigo took another look at the eyes, but they were definitely clear.

"There were a lot of monsters about that day. It was a very strange kind of day. It was the first time I saw the fairies as they really are." She waved her hand in an arc that took in the pond and surrounding area. "They'd been playing games with me, pretending to be dragonflies. That day they let me see their true form."

Okay, thought Indigo recalling Alan's Peter Pan reference, this may not be as helpful as I'd hoped. It sounded like Amy was high as a kite on the day of the murder. Nevertheless, she said, "Tell me about the monsters."

Amy assumed a thoughtful expression, as if she was playing the scene in her mind. "I watched the fairies for ages, maybe hours. It seemed like forever, but it couldn't have been."

She gave a little laugh. "Otherwise I'd still be watching them, wouldn't I? It's difficult to tell how long I was here."

It would be, thought Indigo. If she was as high as she sounded, time would be distorted. "Go on," she said.

"When I left the pond I was feeling really relaxed. Everything was bright and beautiful. I went over onto the heath and walked around for a while, because I wanted to see what that would be like. There were huge, colourful butterflies everywhere and I chased them." She giggled, then recalled something with a grimace and bit at one fingernail. "That's when I saw this fluffy white bunny with blood on its mouth. It was almost as big as me and I knew it must be a were-rabbit, the kind that can turn into a human, and suddenly everything turned dark. All the beautiful colours drained away, which was so sad.

"I didn't like it being dark, so I ran back towards the woods. I thought it would be brighter if I got back to the camp, but the trees tried to stop me. They were scratchy and cruel, and they kept tripping me up. I had to sit down to rest." She fixed Indigo with her eyes and her tone became very matter-of-fact. "That's when the big black spider came along. It had its prey all wrapped up in a cocoon and I watched it put it away to eat later. I kept really still until it had gone away, because I was too tired to run any more.

"Then I got up and walked very carefully, but just before I got back this big black bird swooped down at me. I could tell it wanted to eat me because it was grinning at me. I ran and ran. I was so glad to see the tents. I sat down in the middle of the camp and was very still. I'd almost fallen asleep when Alan came running back and went into his tent. I thought he'd seen the monsters too."

She gave Indigo a beaming smile and nodded firmly. "I know it was that day, because the policemen came."

Indigo was troubled by the story. "Amy," she said gently, "do you have many days like that?"

The girl gave her a very pixyish smile and shook her head. "I know it didn't really happen like that. I'm not as crazy as they say." She toyed with a blade of grass. "It was the joint Toby gave me. He said it was a really amazing one, which would help me see a different world." She gave a sad little sigh that touched Indigo's heart. "I liked the fairies and the butterflies, but the monsters scared me."

"Who's Toby?"

"He was one of the protestors, he's gone now. He said he had this very special weed and I could have some if I let him screw me. I thought it might be fun to see a different world."

Indigo flinched. How often had she heard her runaways tell how they'd been willing to trade sex for booze or a place to sleep? She had a sudden urge to wrap Amy in her arms and take her somewhere safe. Somewhere far away from special joints and people like Toby.

"I don't think that was just weed," she said, "unless it was very strong. Maybe skunk." She reached out and touched the girl's hand. "Can I ask you about the day you first met Peter Taylor?"

"Who?" Amy was staring at Indigo's hand as if she'd never had human contact before and didn't know what to make of it.

Indigo pulled her hand back, half-ashamed of her instinct. "The man who was killed. You and Mike were with Alan in the woods when you met Taylor and a companion. There was an argument."

Amy looked up and nodded. "I remember. They're going to destroy the woods. I was very angry with them."

"Taylor got hit on the nose and knocked down. Do you remember who did that?"

"I did." She bubbled with laughter. "I didn't mean to hit him, he just got too close. Alan tried to stop him getting in the way, but the silly man pulled him down with him."

Indigo nodded absently. All three accounts of that meeting tallied. It looked like Taylor had been wrong to accuse Alan of assaulting him.

"Do you know what happened to the axe that was used to cut firewood?"

"The police kept asking me that. I've tried and tried, but I can't remember. I know I used it. Everyone said I was the last one to use it, but I can't remember. I can't."

She was getting distressed and Indigo again had the urge to put an arm around her, but didn't follow through. Amy was just the sort of lost and aimless young person she'd spent her life trying to help. If nobody put her back on the path to normality soon, she'd drift hopelessly down a bleak tunnel leading to an early death.

"Why are you still here? Almost everyone else has gone."

"I don't have anywhere else to go." She met Indigo's eyes, and there was a kind of pleading in her own. "Besides, it's nice here. It's quiet. I have my pond." She turned back to gaze at the still waters and repeated plaintively, "I have my pond."

Indigo sighed, picked up her phone, stopped the recording, and placed the phone in her pocket. Thanking Amy for talking to her, she scrambled to her feet.

The girl turned back towards her and dug into the folds of her draperies, pulling something from a concealed pocket. Holding it out towards Indigo, she said, "I want you to have my talisman. The fairies blessed it, maybe it will help you set Alan free."

She took the offering and looked down at it. It was a 'Save the Woods' badge, like the one found in Taylor's car. A sudden feeling of appropriateness washed over her, a feeling that the woods held the secret of the murder and might reveal it in exchange for their own safety. Giving a small shake of her head to bat the fantasy away, she gravely thanked Amy, put the badge in her own pocket, and walked away.

Making her way back towards the campsite, she felt heavy and depressed. It didn't seem to matter how many young people she found and returned home, there were always more in need of saving. Alienated, confused, running away from a home they found boring, or running towards some unrealistic dream. She only sought the ones whose families cared enough to pay her to get them back, but she'd encountered plenty who'd run away from bad families and physical or mental abuse. She wondered which category Amy fitted into.

Chapter Five

The campsite looked pretty much the same when she reached it except for the fact that Mike Nash had disappeared and a young black man was sitting outside one of the tents, reading a book. She walked over to him.

"You must be Abiola."

He looked up at her, and she felt as if the bright, intelligent eyes were analysing her, like a laboratory specimen. "I must, and you're the private investigator. Mike told me you were around."

"Do you mind if I ask you some questions?" He shook his head, so she lowered herself to sit opposite him, tapping her phone as she did so. "Were you here on the morning of the murder?"

"At some point." He closed his book and laid it on the ground beside him, giving her his full attention. "My routine has been fairly constant. I take the first bus into town, buy a newspaper, and have breakfast in a café there. That day was no different."

"Do you know what time you got back to camp?"

"Around twenty past nine, perhaps a few minutes later. The nearest bus stop is a little under half a mile from here. I alight there at five past nine every morning." He gave a slightly embarrassed laugh. "You see what a creature of habit I am? But this will interest you, I saw a blue car parked on the verge as I walked back along the road. Before I got near the camp area it started up and drove past me in the direction of town."

She gave a cautious nod, putting a name to one of the statements. "Yes, that would be Taylor's car. You said you didn't see the driver."

"I did not." An expression of regret flitted across his face. "I wasn't looking. I had no reason to notice him, though I berate myself now for being so unobservant."

"You shouldn't beat yourself up over it. You'd be surprised how little people notice of what's happening around them. Was anyone in the camp when you arrived back?"

"Most of them, actually. They were in various stages of preparing and eating breakfast. Personally, I prefer to get a properly cooked meal to start the day." He tapped his forefinger against the cover of his book in an unconscious gesture of reflection. "Amy arrived back shortly after I did. She was shivering and talking to herself. I think she was coming down from something. It seemed very early to be getting high, but I'm just here to observe, so I didn't approach her."

That sounded a strange thing to say. "Observe what?" she asked curiously.

He smiled and pointed to the book. "I'm a postgrad social sciences student. I'm doing a thesis on the dynamics of alternative cultures."

"Such as protest groups?" She took a quick glance at the book and noted its title 'Studies in Group Dynamics'.

"Such as protest groups," he agreed.

"So this is just a project to you? Why didn't you leave when the murder happened?"

The smile widened into a grin. "I have a room on campus, but I have to vacate it during the holidays. Camping in the woods is a cheap way to live. Certainly cheaper than going home to Nigeria for a few weeks. I shall be leaving here at the weekend, ready for the new semester."

Indigo was beginning to appreciate this young man. He seemed the sanest person in this group, and that included her own nephew.

"Did you see Alan Sherman come back into camp?"

"Yes, he came rushing back around ten and scrambled into his tent. He looked upset. I thought maybe he'd quarrelled with his girlfriend."

She blinked, slightly thrown by the sudden introduction of this unexpected element. "Does he have a girlfriend?"

Abiola gave a noncommittal shrug. "I assumed that to be the case. He was always sneaking off into the woods. I took it he was going to meet someone." He hesitated, as if feeling he ought to elaborate. "I suppose it could have been a boyfriend, but I didn't get that vibe from him."

"Did he ever mention anyone?"

"No." His brows furrowed into a frown. "Look, I could have got the whole thing wrong. I might have been letting my studies in human behaviour colour my thinking. It's a danger. Let's just say Alan had some reason or other to go off into the woods alone on a regular basis."

"Was that unusual? I mean, Amy seems to have wandered off alone a lot."

"But she's crazy." He gave a deep peal of laughter. "Sorry, it's the nickname they gave her, Crazy Amy. She's always wandering around in a drug-induced daze. No, Alan left as if he was eager to be somewhere."

She nodded her understanding and filed the information away for later. Might this be the explanation for Alan's vagueness about where he was that morning? How would the existence of a girlfriend affect his defence? Could she give him an alibi? And why on earth would he keep a girlfriend secret from his own family? She thought, guiltily, about the fact that she'd done the same thing with George. Perhaps, like her, Alan had been frightened of jinxing a budding romance. Or maybe Abiola had simply over-analysed the situation.

Turning her attention back to him, she asked, "What about Mike Nash, was he about when you returned?"

"I didn't see him until the police turned up. They practically dragged him out of his tent. He looked really rough. I thought he was going to be sick over them."

"Could he have come back into camp after you did?"

He shook his head with complete confidence. "I was watching them all, with my notebook open, taking notes. I would have noticed Nash coming into camp. He was the group leader. His presence altered the dynamic of the others."

That seemed pretty definite. She thought he was a good observer and he'd had a strong motive to watch his companions.

"One last question," she said. "Do you know what happened to the camp axe?"

"Amy lost it," he replied immediately.

"You're not just saying that because it's what everyone believes?"

"No, I saw it myself. She wandered out of camp swinging it in her hand. I thought she was going for firewood, because there was none left. I was desperate for a cup of coffee and the fire's the best way to boil water. A few of them had those little camping stoves, but they're tricky to use. Besides, the fuel costs money, so they didn't like you borrowing them. When she didn't return, I went to find her. She was standing staring at a tree - no firewood, no axe. I asked her what had happened to it, but she said she must have dropped it. We all looked, but it never turned up."

"I see. Well, thank you."

She scrambled to her feet, thinking that damp grass, hard ground and this getting up and down wasn't as easy to cope with as it once was. Damn it, she was only thirty four, it was too early to be feeling her age. On that depressing thought she made for her car, wondering if that round of interviews had done anything other than confirm what she already knew. Following the dirt track from the campsite brought her to a place where she could see the road through the trees, allowing her to cut through and attain the verge with relative ease compared to her earlier struggle with the undergrowth.

Back in her car, she headed towards Great Oxing, but before inching her way through the narrow Aldgate she diverted to the Aldgate car park, on the outside of the wall. This was where Taylor's car had been found. According to the forensics report the only fingerprints on the wheel belonged to Taylor himself, while smudges showed the killer had worn gloves. Various hairs had been found in the car. Once again these mostly belonged to Taylor, though some had belonged to his colleague Phil Butterworth, and quite a number were from a brown and white Jack Russell Terrier. Apparently, despite his disdain for Nature, Peter Taylor had been a dog owner. Perhaps Mike Nash would have felt less antipathy towards him if he'd known that.

She studied her surroundings. The car park itself was a small one, with bays for only twelve vehicles, all currently empty. Parking was free, so there was no ticket machine, and no CCTV. The tarmac was litter-strewn and surrounded on three sides by tattered commercial buildings. The building on the left was empty and boarded, with a decaying 'To Let' sign still nailed hopefully to the front wall. Across the front of the car park ran a waist high fence of metal tubes with a single gap for both entry and exit. The far end of the street was a respectable small shopping area, but this end had an air of dejected abandonment. It was an ideal place to dump the car, which had remained there for three days until reported by one of their witnesses. She did a U-turn and continued back towards the city, heading for Mrs Hunter, the woman who'd seen the killer in Taylor's car as he'd driven into the car park, and who had alerted the police in response to a televised appeal. Now Indigo had seen the place, she realised how unfortunate he'd been.

Her route took her past the Waterman's Arms and she decided to stop off and verify Nash's story on the way. She knew the place well, since it was one of two locales where they sometimes had the folk bands she liked. As she pulled to a stop she realised the lunchtime crowd hadn't yet dissipated and the place was heaving. Not the best time to try and question the staff, even if they did know her. Since her stomach was telling her it was time to eat, she entered the bar, squeezed herself into an empty seat and ordered some food. Forty minutes later things had quietened down and she was feeling refreshed and ready to return to the fray. As she paid her bill she asked to see the landlord.

Fred Wheeler could have been a model for the ideal barkeep – heavily built, ruddy faced and always cheerful. When he saw who'd asked to see him he gave a massive smile and slid himself carefully into the chair opposite. "Hello Indie, what are you doing here? A bit early for our Thursday night band."

"It's work, not pleasure I'm afraid, Fred. Who was working on the fourth of August?"

He thought for a moment. "I was. Me, Andy and the two girls. What's this about?"

"'Mike Nash, the leader of the 'Save the Trees' group says he was in here that night and got very drunk. I'm just trying to confirm that."

He shook his head doubtfully. "I don't know the name. Maybe if you describe him?"

"Long scraggy hair and beard, Yorkshire accent. Says he got banned."

The man laughed, a roaring kind of laugh so suited to his trade that she sometimes suspected him of cultivating it on purpose. "Oh, I remember him now. He came in a lot up until I banned him. Don't know where he got the money, given he doesn't have a proper job." He absent-mindedly brushed a few crumbs from her table into his hand as he talked. "Yes, he got drunk alright. Worse than usual. Annoyed the hell out of my customers and refused to move at closing time. I had to get Andy to help me get him out the door. That's when I told him not to come back again."

"Can you be sure that was the fourth of August?"

"Oh yes." He nodded emphatically. "For one thing, we had a birthday party going on in the saloon bar and he started sounding off about toffs taking up all the space and forcing the poor bloody working men into a cupboard. Almost threw him out then. He never used the saloon bar, and he doesn't work." He scratched his chin absently. "Besides, when I heard about the murder the next day I said to Renee 'It'll be that bearded guy, you mark my words.' I was surprised when they arrested the other lad."

"What made you think Nash was the killer?"

"What he was saying that night. He was going on and on about the construction people, and how we didn't need more roads. Kept talking about peaked oil or some such. He said it wouldn't be long before there weren't any more cars and all the trees and animals would have died for nothing." He gave another shout of laughter. "He got quite maudlin when he talked about the dead animals, almost made me feel sorry for him. Then he started shouting about how it was the construction people that should be killed and nailed to trees and I had to tell him to keep it down again."

Indigo thanked him, told him she'd try to get to the Thursday gig, and walked back to her car in a thoughtful mood. She felt a sense of frustration. Both Nash and Amy were better candidates for killing Taylor than Alan was, but neither of them fitted Mrs Hunter's description. Besides which, Nash did have a kind of alibi. He was in his tent when the police arrived at the camp, and Abiola had assured her he couldn't have slipped into the tent after dumping Taylor's car without being seen.

Chapter Six

She was still trying to fit either, or both, her suspects into the frame when she arrived at 62 Weymouth Avenue and parked behind a small red car. Mrs Hunter's house was a red-brick mid-terrace with a bay window. She covered the space between the gate and the miniscule porch in three strides, and pushed the doorbell. She half expected to be greeted by a short, wizened, white-haired old lady, but Mrs Hunter was tall, upright and dressed in a well-cut pair of denim jeans, topped by a long colourful blouse. Her bright, intelligent eyes gleamed beneath well-coifed blonde hair as she greeted Indigo. She looked a good ten years younger than her age.

"Ah yes, you're the young lady who rang. Do come in. I've never been interrogated by a private detective before."

"Investigator," murmured Indigo, "I prefer private investigator."

"Do you dear?" Mrs Hunter closed the door and led the way into a neat living room. "I don't suppose there's much difference, is there? I was just about to make myself some tea, I'll get two cups." Without giving her time to answer, she strode away, leaving her alone in the living room.

Indigo looked round and chose an upright grey armchair facing an identical one beside which an open novel lay. She glanced at it and smiled to see it was an Agatha Christie. Perhaps the woman had been checking on the niceties of interrogation techniques.

"So," said the other woman, coming into the room with a tray in her hands, "you say you're working for the youth they've charged with the murder?"

Indigo jumped up, meaning to help her put the tray onto the coffee table, but was waved away. She sat back down and allowed her hostess to perform her duties as she would.

"Actually, it's his mother who hired me," she said, having decided to keep her relationship to Alan out of things unless it looked like it would be helpful.

"Ah," said Mrs Hunter, "now that makes sense. Mothers do that kind of thing, don't they?" She handed Indigo a cup of tea and offered biscuits, which were declined. "I know I'd do anything to help either of my sons."

There was something about her tone which made Indigo think this a conditional statement. She suspected the sons in question would be in some trouble if they got themselves into a situation like Alan's. "Then you won't mind answering a few questions?"

"Of course not, that's why I agreed to meet you. Fire away." The woman nodded, like a teacher encouraging a pupil to speak. "Though I don't know whether my answers will be of any use to you."

"Do you mind if I record the interview?"

An odd smile flickered across the other's features. "That's what the police do, isn't it? Yes, I think I'd prefer a record of my actual words."

Wondering what was behind the strange response, Indigo tapped her phone and placed it on the arm of her chair. "Now, Mrs Hunter, could you just tell me what happened that morning?"

"I had a doctor's appointment," she replied promptly. "That's how I came to be in the car park. My appointment was for nine o'clock. I like to get a morning appointment, there's less chance of them running late and keeping you waiting. I was pretty well on time that day. I got back to my car about nine thirty and drove out of the car park just as the blue car was driving in."

"You saw the driver?"

"I certainly did." She emphasised the statement with a decisive nod. "The young man had very bad manners. I was just about to drive through the gate when he arrived and he didn't wait for me to get out. He must have been just inches away from my right wing. I thought for a moment he was going to hit me, but I gave him a good hard glare and he swung away."

"You described him as young and fair?"

Mrs Hunter tutted and treated Indigo to an example of her glare. "I did not describe him as fair at all, I said he had brown hair. That wretched policeman kept on at me about the colour, suggesting I might have been dazzled by sunlight. I told him no, it was definitely brown. He tried to get me to be more accurate about the shade and I said mid-brown. That's when he said 'Let's call it fair, shall we?'." The intelligent eyes flashed anger momentarily. "Some people patronise you when you're old. He was so determined to have it as fair that in the end I left him to it."

She gave a deep sigh and looked down at her teacup. "It was wrong of me, of course, but I could see he wasn't going to let me go until I agreed with him." She looked up and met Indigo's eyes frankly. "That's why I decided to talk to you. If they've arrested that young man on the basis of his hair colour, then I don't want that on my conscience."

Indigo was startled. "But this is terrible. Are you saying Inspector Howard intimidated a witness?"

"Oh it wasn't the Inspector. The first interview was with a young woman, a police constable I think. Then they asked me to come back and talk to the ... SPO?"

"SIO? Chief Inspector Waters?"

"That's the man. He kept telling me what an important witness I was."

Indigo found herself smiling. "In-between trying to get you to change your statement?"

The bright eyes twinkled in response. "Exactly." She gave a frustrated sigh. "I shouldn't have caved in, should I? But he was so very persistent, and I was supposed to be meeting up with a friend that afternoon."

"I see." Indigo suddenly did begin to understand and her heart sank. A picture was emerging of Waters seizing the most useful evidence and creating a case out of it. The t-shirt with the wrong amount of blood, the hair colour that didn't quite match what was required. It sounded suspiciously like the DCI was adjusting the facts to fit his suspect. Whether it was deliberate or unconscious, she couldn't tell yet, but it was certainly bad policing. Was that why George had been reluctant to talk about the case? If there was one thing she knew about her ex-lover, it was his complete probity in all things.

She realised she couldn't rely on anything in Mrs Hunter's written statement and, recalling the way the woman had called her young lady when she arrived, she played a hunch. "When you say the man was young, what age do you mean, exactly?"

"Oh, no more than forty."

Indigo had been holding the teacup and sipping out of it intermittently, but the reply was so surprising she put the cup down on the coffee table and leant forward. "Forty? I wouldn't have called that young."

The other woman smiled slightly. "But you're younger than that yourself, aren't you? My eldest grandson's about your age and I still think of him as young."

"Could the driver have been a lot younger? Say, nineteen?"

"Good heavens, no. I wouldn't have described a nineteen-year-old as a man, no matter how low they make the voting age. As far as I'm concerned, my grandsons are boys until they reach twenty one." She put down her cup and straightened her shoulders against the upright chair back. "That line up was full of teenage boys. I tried to tell them then they had it all wrong."

I'll bet you did, thought Indigo, and the DCI probably patted you on the head and told you to leave it to them. "If he couldn't have been more than forty," she probed, "what's the youngest he could have been?"

"That's a tricky one," the woman admitted, retrieving her cup. She glanced at a family photograph on the wall, as if that could help her answer the question. "Thirty, maybe. Not much younger than that, I shouldn't have thought."

"I see. Didn't you tell this to Inspector Waters?"

Mrs Hunter gave a regretful sigh. "He didn't ask," she said, "and it didn't occur to me to be that precise about the age at the time. I do think I may have said to him 'about your age' at one point, but perhaps he didn't hear me."

Didn't want to hear, more like, Indigo thought. She felt both optimism and pessimism rise within her and clash inharmoniously. The key witness was describing someone very different from Alan Sherman. That would help Dawson and the barrister prepare their defence, but that was for the future. In the meantime, the DCI in charge of the case was blindly pursuing his own version of the truth, which meant it would be very difficult to make him drop Alan and look elsewhere. Especially since he now seemed to consider the matter closed. Pessimism won. It began to look like the only way to get her nephew out of jail quickly might, indeed, be to catch the real culprit.

"And it was definitely a man?" she asked hopefully. "It couldn't have been a woman?"

The bright eyes sparkled with amusement. "I'm not so old I can't tell the difference."

Indigo blushed and shook her head. "Sorry, but so much of that statement's wrong I thought I'd better ask." She picked up her phone, turned off the record mode, and rose to her feet, putting out a hand.

Mrs Hunter shook it firmly and led the way back to the front door. At the door, Indigo stopped and met the intelligent eyes frankly. "I understand what you meant about the police recording now. Yes, I'm sure the defence can get that entered as evidence."

"I thought they might, but thank you for giving me the chance to put the record straight. I'd have said all that in court, you know, regardless of what I signed. It's been troubling me ever since I attended that line-up and saw they were going the wrong way."

As she drove away, Indigo realised she was a little disappointed Amy had been ruled out. How simple it would have been if Crazy Amy had killed Taylor with the missing axe, mistaking him for a monster whilst in a drug-induced bout of paranoia. She sighed. Somehow, she was pretty sure that shrewd elderly woman would have spotted a pixy faced girl with green hair. Get a grip on yourself, woman, she chided. You're as bad as Chief Inspector Waters, looking for the easy answer.

The afternoon was getting on and Indigo had no more interviews planned so she headed back to the agency. Maisie looked up from her computer screen as she entered the outer office.

"How did it go?" she asked. "I can't tell from your expression whether it was good or bad."

"Confusing," replied Indigo. "Any messages?"

"Jack called from Birmingham. They want him to stay another week. He asked if you needed him back here."

"That's the chemical company job?" Maisie nodded. "He can stay. Rupert can handle the few other bits we've got on while I'm doing this. Anything else?"

"Your sister rang."

"Already? I've barely started."

"It's her son, pet, she's anxious. I would be too, in her place."

"I know, I know, but I don't want to give her daily updates. This is going to be a roller-coaster ride. I certainly don't want to take her along with me. She's in such a state already she'll only get depressed by the setbacks."

"How about I give her the daily updates? You know how good I am at saying nothing and making it sound optimistic. Let me do the customer service bit and you go rescue her son."

Indigo gave a reluctant nod of agreement. "I suppose someone needs to hold her hand. I'll be in the conference room if anyone wants me."

Conference room was a rather grand name for the room they used for meetings and discussions. Its long, narrow shape made it unsuitable for use as an office, so it housed a table and four chairs, a whiteboard that could be used as a screen for the overhead projector, three filing cabinets full of archived cases and a bookcase stacked with reference books. Since they were rarely all in the office together there were few staff meetings, but the room was a good place to eat lunch when there was time to relax.

She cleaned the whiteboard off carefully, then stood in front of it with a marker in her hand. The time and place grid she used to track down missing people wasn't going to help in this case. Or was it? Maybe a modified version would help sort out alibis, but she was nowhere near being ready for that yet. Eventually she decided on another kind of grid. On the left she listed everything they knew about the killer – Age, gender, race, etc. – forming a column. Then she created further columns, each with a name at the top, and filled in the relevant information about each person. So far, she had four names; Alan, Mike Nash, Amy and Abiola. None of them really fitted the picture she was building of the killer, especially now the age was given as thirty to forty.

She'd just finished the grid when there was a knock at the door and she called "Come in."

The young man who bounced into the room reminded her a little of her nephew, but only by virtue of his age. Rupert Gray was a bright, confident twenty two year old with loads of enthusiasm. His curly auburn hair was always unruly, his green eyes always shone. He could get down from time to time, but never stayed that way for long and he was far too persistent to ever feel defeated.

She smiled to herself as she remembered just how persistent he could be. He'd turned up at the agency asking her to train him. He told her he'd work for free, but he wasn't the first person to make that offer, and probably wouldn't be the last. Some people think the life of a private detective is glamorous and exciting, and sometimes they approach working PIs as a way in. She'd done what she usually did, explained the realities, told him where he could get training if he was willing to pay for it, and told him she had no vacancies. A few months later he was back with a certificate in his hand, still willing to work for free. She kept putting him off and he kept coming back. In the end she offered to give him a two month trial, expecting him to drop out once he realised how deadly boring the work could be. He'd not only stuck it out, but shown the potential to be a good investigator, so she'd caved in and given him a job. That was eighteen months ago and she wasn't sorry she'd taken the chance.

Now he stood looking at the whiteboard with interest. "Hi boss, can I help?"

"The Mystery Shopper job?"

"I've done the first batch of stores. The report's on your desk." He nodded towards the grid. "Is this the murder case?"

"Yes."

"I've read the police reports."

So that was it, Rupert wanted in on the murder investigation. "I suppose Maisie gave you the reports?" Her PA had taken Rupert under her wing from his first entry into the agency and was always trying to find opportunities for him to shine.

He grinned and cocked his head to one side. "She might have accidentally left the USB stick on her desk."

"Rupert, you're incorrigible. And you shouldn't encourage Maisie to aid and abet you."

"She enjoys it." He gave her a wink. "I think she's adopted me."

She snorted and shook her head. "You, young man, take advantage of women's maternal instincts. You'd better make the most of it while you're still young enough to do so."

"I plan to segue seamlessly from ingénue to mature charmer." He nodded towards the grid she'd written on the whiteboard. "Mike Nash is the only one who fits the description of the killer."

"He has an alibi, and he says he can't drive."

"You sound like you don't believe him." He frowned at the board. "You're sure he's got an alibi?"

"It's not watertight," she admitted, "but it's reasonable. I trust Abiola to have spotted him if he'd come into camp after nine twenty."

"How long would it take to walk from the car park to the campsite?"

"Walk? I don't know. It's about five and a half miles."

"That's over an hour, even at a fast walking pace. You could probably do it in under an hour if you ran. I could try it out."

She pretended not to have heard the offer. "Nash was in no state to do any running that morning. God alone knows how he got back the night before. There's a bus stop within half a mile of the camp, but he couldn't have killed Taylor and beaten Abiola back to camp, because Abiola saw the killer driving Taylor's car away" She flopped down on a chair and stared at the board. "Besides which, Nash has a beard. I'm pretty sure

Mrs Hunter would have mentioned something that noticeable. Let's face it, Rupert, we've no real suspects at the moment."

He remained standing and turned to face her. "There were a lot of other people in the camp at the time of the murder. I could track them down for you. The police took all their names and addresses."

"I doubt if they'd give them to you," she said absently, trying to think things through. "They're funny about addresses. The thing is, I'm not convinced this is anything to do with the protestors. Nobody else in the camp had even met Taylor, and he was only a consultant. It would have made more sense to kill one of the H&G managers, or someone in the actual construction crew." Her forehead wrinkled as she stared unseeingly at the board. "Mind you, they haven't even reached the woods yet." She gave a slow shake of her head. "No, the body was dumped where it was to point the finger at the protest camp. There's got to be a different motive somewhere."

"Okay, boss," he agreed readily, "but where do you look next?"

She continued her unfocused staring, absently tapping the fingers of her right hand against the table. "Henckle and Green," she said finally. "Alan's badge wasn't the only thing found in Taylor's car. There was a Henckle and Green security pass belonging to one Philip Butterworth. The police did a cursory interview with Taylor's boss, but I don't think they spoke to anyone else at the firm. At least, I didn't see any witness statements belonging to co-workers."

She got to her feet, pushing her chair under the table. "I'll get Maisie to make me an appointment with Eleanor Knight, Taylor's boss. After that, I'll play it by ear."

"And if that doesn't get you anywhere?" he asked as she walked towards the door.

She half-turned and gave a resigned shrug. "Then I go on to Taylor's friends and family. He must have known his killer, only serial killers murder strangers." She saw a look of speculation enter his eyes and laughed. “No, Rupert, we’re not dealing with a serial killer. Look, when I get something you can help me with, I’ll call you. Okay?”

Chapter Seven

Indigo's appointment with Eleanor Knight was for ten o'clock the next day. She arrived promptly and was asked to wait in the lobby until someone came down to collect her. It gave her the chance to assess the brand new offices, built by Henckle and Green themselves as a showcase of their work. She managed to be both impressed and unimpressed at the same time. The work was smooth and professional. Glass and metal gleamed appropriately. The mock leather seating was comfortable, without being luxurious. But it was all so predictable. There wasn't one iota of original thought or daring innovation in the whole building.

She was saved from the uncomfortable feeling she'd landed in an out-of-town shopping mall by the arrival of Eleanor Knight's PA, who introduced herself as Janice. The woman was in her late twenties, attractive rather than pretty, but well dressed and made up. It took Indigo less than sixty seconds to work out she had ambitions, but not the mental or social skills needed to realise them. As they travelled up to the marketing suite in the lift, she tried a little delicate pumping.

"I understand Mr Taylor worked with Phil Butterworth," she said conversationally. "How did they get on?"

Janice threw her a look of complete confusion. "Alright, I guess. Mostly." For a moment she fidgeted as if in discomfort, then added. "You know, don't you? About Phil getting told off?"

Indigo suppressed a smile and tried an old ploy. She bent towards the younger woman and lowered her voice. "Oh, yes, but I didn't realise it was widely known."

At that point the lift stopped and there was an unfortunate break in conversation as they exited and walked from the lift lobby into an open area where a desk was set diagonally in one corner. Indigo glanced at the filing cabinets, the printer, and the row of visitor chairs and guessed this was the PA's domain. Janice pointed to the seating and offered coffee, saying Eleanor was engaged with another visitor at present. She declined the drink, fearing she'd lost momentum on the questioning. She needn't have worried. The younger woman hovered, and finally spoke in a rush.

"If Phil wanted it kept quiet, he shouldn't have gone around shouting his mouth off, should he? I mean, Mr Taylor tried to be discreet. He told him off behind closed doors, like. It wasn't his fault Miss Knight walked in on them just as he was calling Phil lazy and useless. If that had happened to me, I wouldn't go around telling everyone."

"No, of course not. But perhaps Phil felt the criticism was unfair?"

"He was furious. He said they'd brought Taylor in to help pin the whole Route Two thing on him."

"And did they?"

Janice narrowed her eyes and gave her a look that told her not to be so silly. "They brought him in to clear up Phil's mess, didn't they? I mean, Phil was bid manager. He's the one what got the costs wrong and now the company's going to lose money. It's only natural everyone's angry with him."

Indigo nodded, conveying her total understanding. "Remind me about Route Two," she prompted.

"Route Two's the bypass route. You know, the one the council changed after they accepted Phil's bid. Mr Taylor was going to get the council to pay us more money. Now he's dead, Miss Knight is having to deal with them." She nodded towards the closed door across from them. "She's talking to Mr Winslow from the council right now. He's in charge of planning and regeneration." She pronounced the words carefully, like something she wasn't totally sure of. "I like him, he's always nice to me, but I don't think he's going to give us more money."

As if she'd spoken a cue line, the door opened and a man and woman came out.

Winslow was an attractive man in his mid-thirties, dressed in a smart charcoal grey suit which fitted his slim frame perfectly. It was of extremely good quality, as was the narrow black leather briefcase he carried. As he shook hands with Eleanor Knight a flash of gold at his wrist showed he was wearing cufflinks. Turning to leave he nodded briefly to Indigo, then gave Janice a charm-filled smile and bade her goodbye. Indigo was intrigued. His entire appearance and demeanour was a studied example of executive poise, but to her mind there was something a little too studied about it. Now, why would a local government officer want to portray himself as a successful businessman? Was it just to impress the private sector managers he had to deal with?

She turned towards Eleanor Knight, who was nearly a decade older than the council man. The woman was standing in the doorway of her office, a scowl fading from her face. She was tall and blonde, but her pretty features were marred by prominent front teeth. Even as she stood with her lips partially closed, her top teeth stuck out noticeably over the bottom ones. She wore a mid-blue suit with a pencil skirt, revealing a taut body that had undoubtedly taken hours of gym work to achieve. Another person striving to bolster their management ambitions by the front they projected. Indigo glanced down at her own jeans and was glad she didn't work in that kind of environment. Still, those teeth spoilt the whole effect, she should really have them fixed.

Once Winslow had disappeared from sight, Eleanor Knight shook herself and turned in Indigo's direction.

"Miss Lattimer?" she asked, holding the door wide. "Come in. I'm sorry to keep you."

The Marketing Manager's office was remarkably impersonal. True, there were framed diplomas and awards on the wall, but no photos, no art, no knickknacks, nor anything else that showed the kind of person Eleanor Knight was. A large plant in a fancy pot stuck in a corner of the room was merely living furniture. How sad, Indigo thought, remembering her own treasured antiques. Fancy spending so much of your day surrounded by blandness. She must really be focussed on her career.

The impression was heightened by the way the woman dropped into the seat behind her desk and said, "God, I hate patronising men."

"Bad meeting?"

The other laughed and tried to cover her lack of discretion. "I should be used to it. The construction industry's still very much a man's world."

"But he's a local government officer. I thought the public sector was more female friendly."

"You wouldn't know it from talking to Derian Winslow. Mind you, we are in the middle of a contract challenge, so I don't suppose I can expect him to be sweetness and light." She straightened in her seat and pushed the papers on her desk to one side. "Now, how can I help you?"

"My PA will have told you I'm working for Mrs Sherman. She's hired me to help prepare the defence case. I'd like to get some background information on Peter Taylor and the work he was doing here."

Eleanor frowned and picked up a biro, which she began to tap mechanically against her desk. "I agreed to meet with you, but I'm not sure whether I really want to help the defence. I feel rather responsible for what happened to Peter. After all, it was me who brought him to Great Oxing in the first place."

So, it was like that? But then, working for the defence was never going to be easy. Time for a little bluntness. That would be the best approach with a woman like this. "Don't you believe in the British justice system?"

That startled her, as it was meant to. She pulled back a little and her eyes widened. "Of course I do."

"Then you'll agree the accused is entitled to the best defence possible." Indigo stretched out her hand, palm up. "I'm not out to denigrate Taylor, or suggest he brought about his own death. I just need to know what sort of a person he was, what his job entailed. That kind of thing."

"Well, I suppose that's not an unreasonable thing to ask." She still seemed hesitant but, after a moment, sighed and said, "Okay. You ask questions and I'll do my best to answer them. If I think you're being inappropriate, I'll tell you so."

"Thank you." Indigo had her phone in her left hand. It had been recording ever since her first question to Janice. She now laid it casually on the edge of the desk, as if freeing her hands to talk. "How long had Taylor been employed by H&G?"

"He wasn't an employee, he was a planning consultant. I hired him in June, shortly after the Council altered the bypass route and refused to let us raise our fees."

"I take it this is what the contract challenge is about. Why do you need to raise your fees?"

Eleanor showed irritation, though Indigo couldn't tell whether it was aimed at her or Oxely District Council. "Because the council has increased our construction costs by changing part of the bypass route. We bid on the route as it was described in the tender documents. Then, after we'd already begun construction on the initial stage of the road, their Executive Member for Regeneration agreed a change to the section along Oxley Woods. It wasn't originally meant to go through the woodland at all. It was meant to take a swathe out of the golf course." She began tapping the pen again, rapidly. "Have you any idea how much time and effort it takes to clear that much mature woodland? If I can't get the Council to back down, we'll actually lose money on this contract."

"Surely the contract allows you to recover any additional costs caused by alterations in the route?"

"Only if they affect a stretch greater than ten miles long. The Oxley Woods change falls short of that." She stopped tapping and threw the pen onto her desk, where it rolled to the edge and fell to the floor with a clatter. "That idiot Butterworth. God alone knows what he was thinking, letting that clause into the contract."

Indigo was still puzzled, though the reference to Butterworth made her think they were heading in the right direction. She gave a delicate cough. "I'm still not sure I understand how the additional costs can cause H&G to lose money. You must have had some contingency." She saw the gleam in Eleanor's eye and faltered. "What about your profit margin? Won't that cushion you?"

The other woman shook her head but didn't answer.

Indigo took a guess. "Does all this have to do with the confrontation between Taylor and Butterworth?"

Eleanor blinked. "My, you are well informed." She hesitated, and Indigo could see her weighing up whether to expose the company's dirty laundry. Eventually she decided to spill the lot. "It's rather embarrassing, but yes. I let Phil Butterworth have his head on this contract. It was his first solo effort as bid manager." She gave a very deep sigh. "To be honest, we didn't stand a chance in hell of getting the contract, so I thought it would be good practice for him. We were up against big competition."

Indigo had an epiphany. "Butterworth underbid everyone," she said.

"It's my own fault, I should have checked his figures more carefully. I just made sure they were within the guidelines. It's true they were brushing the lower limit, but I honestly wasn't expecting us to win the contract, even with a low bid."

"You could have pulled out once you realised the profit margin was too low."

"Too low? It was non-existent." Eleanor gritted her prominent teeth, giving a brief impression of a bulldog. "No, that's not fair. There was a very small profit, and Butterworth was right to argue the prestige was worth a lot. Pulling out after we'd won the contract would have harmed our reputation, made us look like amateurs."

Indigo took a deep breath and tried to tread very carefully, realising the other woman's agitation had caused her to reveal a lot more than she'd needed to. "So what, precisely, did Taylor tell Butterworth off about?"

"Oh, he told him he'd been sloppy. He hadn't done a risk analysis, or included that contingency you mentioned. He'd made no allowance for anything like this route change to occur. Peter thought it was criminal carelessness."

"What did you expect Taylor to do about the situation?"

"He was an ex council officer himself. He'd been Head of Planning somewhere in Surrey. I wanted him to go through all the documents and plans to see if there was any way we could get back on track, financially."

"And was there?"

"Well," she drew the word out to its full length. "Peter was very concerned about the way the change of route had been agreed. Just a few days before his death he told me he thought we could get the council to revert back to the original plans. Not really what I wanted, because I was hoping to improve on Butterworth's profit margin, but better than making a loss."

"How was he going to do that?"

Eleanor shook her head. "I've no idea. He just said the whole thing was unsatisfactory. I know he was preparing a report to put before the planning committee, but he said —"

she hesitated. "I can't quite remember. He said he'd had dealings with them before and they were untrustworthy."

"What, all of them?" asked Indigo, suddenly wondering if Taylor was prone to conspiracy theories.

"No, just one person. I don't know who. To be honest, I wasn't paying full attention. Peter could drone on about planning regulations and committee meetings like a typical bureaucrat. I don't understand the workings of local government, that's why I got him in. So I sometimes switched off when he was in full flow. Now I feel guilty about it, of course."

She stopped speaking and frowned thoughtfully. Indigo realised there was more to come and waited patiently for her to resume, which she did at a slower pace. "The route change was signed off by Councillor Porter, who's head of the planning committee, but Peter might have been talking about any of the committee members. I got the impression he thought he could force the full committee to override Porter's decision. He said there was something improper about the way in which the agreement had been reached, but he didn't explain what it was. I thought they'd probably breached some council protocol or other. They have some rather arcane rules in local government." She gave a sigh of regret. "I wish he hadn't kept so much in his head. I'll probably never know what they did wrong now."

She lapsed into silence again, this time signalling the end of her answer. Indigo tried a different tack. "What sort of person was Peter Taylor?"

Once again, Eleanor hesitated. "I don't want you to take this the wrong way, but he wasn't a sociable person. He was very good at detail, perhaps a bit too good. He did like to have everything neat and tidy. He could be pedantic, and that upset some people."

"Was he argumentative? Exacting? Butterworth seems to have thought he was unfair."

"Butterworth deserved that telling off, and it wasn't Peter's fault everyone knew about it. I accidentally walked in on them and Butterworth was so upset he sounded off to all his colleagues. Which only made him look worse. If he'd kept quiet, no one would have known. I certainly wouldn't have said anything.

"No, Peter wasn't particularly argumentative, but he was ... disappointed. I don't think he wanted to leave the public sector. I think he'd been made redundant. He made some bitter comment once about being pensioned off."

Indigo nodded, deciding she had all she needed from Eleanor, but couldn't see that any of it was going to help her. Except, maybe, the set up with Phil Butterworth. She asked if Eleanor would object to her talking to Butterworth, and got her okay.

"By the way," she asked, as she was getting out of her chair, "what reason did the council give for changing the route?"

The other tutted impatiently. "Oh, it was silly. The owner of the Country Club was appealing the Compulsory Purchase Order for his bit of land. They argued it would save time to go through the woodland since the Council already own it and there would be no appeal process."

"And won't it?"

"Of course not. Even Butterworth knew enough to take the CPO process into account when drawing up the plans. People are always appealing. It would have been all over by the time we got as far as the Country Club and Spencer-Cooper had very little chance of winning. As it is, it's going to take us extra time to clear the woodland before we can even start levelling the ground and constructing the road."

Eleanor Knight walked her to the door and pointed the way across the corridor to the office Phil Butterworth shared with the other three members of the marketing team. Before shaking her hand, Eleanor laughed and said, "Do you know, the

Council even want us to dig up the existing road along the woods. Now that I can charge them for, because it wasn't included in the original plans."

Chapter Eight

The marketing team shared an office not much bigger than Eleanor Knight's. This room, however, contained six desks. A group of four to the right of the door held three male workers. The other two were facing a wall to the left, but only one was occupied. Indigo closed the door behind her and said "Phil Butterworth?" to the office at large. The lone worker looked up and one of the others pointed mutely in his direction. She walked over towards him, wondering why he hadn't moved to the unused desk among the four. It didn't take her long to understand the psychology that placed him in the worst position in the room. He was awkward, clumsy and self-conscious.

Whereas Eleanor's prettiness was spoilt only by her prominent teeth, Butterworth was unfortunate on all fronts. His watery blue eyes seemed unable to rest on anything for long, making him appear shifty. His hair was thin and lifeless, the colour that indeterminate shade of brown often referred to as mouse. When he rose to greet her, knocking a stapler onto the floor as he did so, she could see his cheap suit hung unkindly on his gangly body. He failed to meet her eyes when they shook hands, and knocked several more items of stationery to the floor as he tried to retrieve the stapler.

Afraid the computer terminal might go flying if he sought a chair for her, she quickly retrieved the one from the unused desk and placed it beside his. She wasn't sure whether the nerviness was natural, or whether he was feeling guilty about something. If it was about the murder, maybe she could make him nervous enough to confess.

Once they were seated calmly, and all his equipment was restored to its place on his desk, she introduced herself and explained her mission. "I understand you worked closely with Peter Taylor?" she said. "Maybe you could tell me a little bit about him? What kind of person he was, what he did here at H&G?"

"Oh." He licked at his lips and stared past her right ear. "Well. I mean, I liked Taylor. He was a good guy. Very professional. He had lots of experience. He understood all the local authority stuff, which was a great help." He laughed, waved a hand, and very nearly knocked the stapler off his desk again. "A pity he wasn't here when I put the bid together. I mean, his knowledge would have helped me with the tender documents and all that."

She wasn't fooled by the enthusiasm. Raising a doubtful eyebrow, she finally managed to make eye contact. "So, exactly what was Mr Taylor's role?"

"He —" Butterworth shifted his head to avoid her gaze and took a couple of deep breaths. "He was supposed to help us persuade Oxely District Council to give us more money," he said in a rush. Then, despite his best efforts, his true feelings bled through and his voice turned petulant. "They changed the route."

He suddenly leant forward with his elbows on the desk and finally met her eyes voluntarily, his own dark and brooding. "It wasn't my fault. How was I supposed to guess the damned council were going to change the route? It's alright the bosses saying I underpriced the contract, but I followed the guidelines. H&G wasn't the natural choice, you know. We were up against some big hitters. I only got it because I cut the costs to the bone. They ought to have congratulated me. It's a big contract. It's worth a little loss to get the bypass under our belt."

"But Peter Taylor didn't see it like that, did he? He said some pretty nasty things to you."

It's quite rare to see someone go bright red in real life, but Phil Butterworth managed it in a matter of seconds. "He had no right to say what he did. He wasn't my boss. He was just a consultant. He had no right."

"You were very angry about it, I hear."

Sensing danger, he sat up, dropped his eyes from hers again, and quickly changed the subject. "I was there, you know. When Taylor met those protestors in the woods. When he got knocked over."

Indigo was willing to let the conversation go where he led. His evasion of her question had been as good an answer as any he could have put into words. "Were you?" she said. "Why don't you tell me about it."

"We went out there because Taylor wanted to see where the road was due to go. We were just walking along the route." He glanced up, a grimace flitting across his face as he recalled the day. "It wasn't easy, cause it's all trees and bushes and brambles and things. I wasn't really dressed for that kind of trek. Anyway, these protestors just appeared on the path ahead of us."

"How many?"

"Three. The guy they've arrested, this weird girl with green hair, and a big bully of a bloke with a beard." He shivered and glanced towards the door as if checking his escape route. "I don't know why they arrested the young one. He was more or less normal."

"But the others weren't?"

"Not on your life. The girl was totally mad. She kept shouting at us and waving a huge stick around. It was her that hit Taylor, not the other one. If the police had asked me, I would have told them."

"The police didn't talk to you?"

"No."

"Do you think the girl could have killed Taylor?" She asked the question to try and keep him focused, since he was giving every indication of a desire to bolt for safety. It was obvious the whole subject of Taylor's death unsettled him.

The ploy seemed to work, for he stared back at a spot just past her right ear and thought for a moment. "My money's on the bearded guy," he said at last.

"Mike Nash."

"Is that his name? He was really threatening. He told Taylor someone should put him down like people did to innocent animals."

"Really? What made him say that?" she asked, wondering if his account would tally with Nash's own.

Butterworth looked at her in genuine surprise. "I forgot, you never met Taylor, did you? He loved concrete and glass and shiny steel. When we were walking through the woods, he had his nose all wrinkled. Like the place smelled. Which it didn't, only leaf mould and pine. He hated the natural world and he said so to that Nash character."

"I see."

She thought for a moment. Butterworth had confirmed the details of the meeting in the woods as she'd obtained them from all the other parties, but it hadn't taken her any further forward. She decided to push him back into the danger zone.

"Did you know your office pass was found in Mr Taylor's car after the murder?"

That caught him off guard. He gulped, his Adam's apple bobbing noticeably up and down. "Was it? I wondered where that had gone. I thought I'd dropped it in the street. I had to get a replacement."

"Have you any idea how it got there?"

"It must have fallen out of my pocket when I was in his car." Both voice and eyes pleaded with her to believe him. "We always took his car if we went anywhere together. I guess mine was too untidy for him."

She nodded, then slipped in a killer question. "And where were you on the morning of the fifth of August around nine o'clock?"

He answered without any of the hesitation or uncertainty he'd previously shown. "I was visiting one of our sites over in Nunsfield. It's on Stanford Street. We're converting an old pub into flats."

"You're sure it was that day and time?"

"Oh yes."

Well, thought Indigo as she got herself together and said goodbye, when someone can give you an alibi like that without thinking about it, it usually means they've prepared it in advance. Now, why would Phil Butterworth prepare himself an alibi for the time of Taylor's murder? His hair is brownish, and he's getting on for thirty. Could he be a suspect? He was certainly angry with Taylor for the telling off, but was that enough motive for a vicious murder?

She was so impressed with Butterworth's pre-prepared alibi she decided to check it out. It meant driving over to Nunsfield to talk to the people at the construction site, but that wasn't too much of a chore and she could swing past home on the way back and prepare herself some lunch for once.

She drove the western route from Great Oxing to Nunsfield. It meant edging through Aldgate again, but allowed her to drive down the country lane past the woods near where Taylor's body had been found. The glorious summer had now definitely turned into autumn, and the deciduous trees were shedding their leaves. To Indigo it was as if they were crying great, drifting, brown tears. Though whether over the death that had occurred beneath them, or the fate which would tear some of them from the ground before summer returned again, she couldn't be sure.

She hated the thought of a massive four-lane carriageway being built anywhere through here, disturbing this typically tranquil English scene. Even the glimpses of golf course she got through the Country Club trees promised peace and relaxation from a crazy world. For a moment she totally understood Mike Nash's position. A deep love and respect for Nature. She began to wonder what she'd have thought of Peter K. Taylor if they'd ever met.

She reached Stanford Street a little before one and easily found the old pub that was being converted into flats. There was hoarding around it with the obligatory notices about hard hats, and signs proclaiming Henckle and Green's motto to 'Build Tomorrow Today'. Not wanting to blunder around a building site without the required safety protection, it took her a while to find somebody to talk to. It seemed most of the men were at lunch, but she was directed to the site office where the site foreman was poring over plans. She asked him about Phil Butterworth.

He sucked a tooth as he thought. "I know Phil Butterworth, yes," he said. "And he did come out here one day last month. I can't place the day, though."

"It would have been a Tuesday. The first one in August."

He thought about it for a while. "Could be. Yes, that's right. We were just laying some concrete and I was annoyed at the interruption."

"That was early in the morning, around nine?"

His eyes narrowed briefly, then he shook his head. "It must have been about eleven. He had a very smart suit on, I recall, not the kind you want to wear on a building site. I did wonder if he had a lunch date and was just killing time. He didn't have any reason to be here, you see. He poked around for a few minutes, asked silly questions and left."

She frowned at him, not quite sure she understood. "Why didn't he have a reason to be here?"

The foreman grinned and raised an eyebrow. "He's marketing, right? His job's done once we have the contract. There's no call for him to be coming round to any of the sites.

God knows what he wanted, but he's Head Office, so you have to be polite."

"Yes, of course."

She thanked him and returned to her car, taking the eastern route back towards Great Oxing. She followed the main A road for a while, then turned onto a B road which skimmed that side of Oxley Woods. Both these roads had been unsuitably placed to form part of the bypass, for which she was grateful, since her little house was situated alongside the B road surrounded by woodland. It was this that had made her encourage her nephew in his desire to join the protestors. In some ways she considered the woods an extension of her home, a place of calm and contemplation.

Her home, which she referred to as 'the cabin', had once been Oxley Woods railway station, a small country station with two short platforms, each of which had contained basic buildings. The line had survived Dr Beeching's cuts in the sixties, but had succumbed to falling custom thirty years later. She'd bought the place at a bargain price, turned the main building into a home for herself, and converted the waiting room area on the far platform into a kind of studio flat, in case of visitors. At the moment it was occupied by Rupert as part of his salary.

Since she was only stopping for a quick lunch she didn't bother putting her car in the garage, but parked beside it and walked down the earthen path. The main building glittered before her, it's full length picture windows and sliding glass doors reflecting the afternoon sunlight. Behind all the glass was a kind of sun lounge which looked out across her sunken garden towards the other platform and the studio. At the right hand end of the platform the original green painted footbridge still rose up as a means of getting from one platform to the other. Behind the far platform elders and buddleia marked the beginning of the woodland, which also encroached at the sides, being kept out of her garden by sturdy brown fences. The effect was to make her home a little oasis, attached to the outside world only by the quiet B road running past the front.

As she unlocked the glass doors a small black shape darted out of the shadows and wrapped itself around her ankles. She looked down. "Oh, we're hungry today, are we Midnight? No luck with the hunting, or have you been too lazy to try?"

It was a foolish question. She'd come across the cat as a half-starved, bedraggled wreck lying in her garden some three years before. She suspected it had once been owned and pampered, but had been thrown out to fend for itself, a task at which it was extremely bad. She'd had a stark choice – take care of it or let it die. The initial arrangement between them had been simple. She put down water, but only gave food when it seemed necessary. The cat was supposed to catch what it could, but it began asking for food more and more often and she'd weakened. Now, she fed it regularly when she was home, and allowed it to sleep inside the house. When she was away on a search, Rupert saw to its dietary needs.

Not wanting to let Midnight inside when she was intending to go out again, she left her sitting hopefully on the platform and went straight to her tiny kitchen. She prepared food for the cat first, knowing that would keep her from pawing at the door. Once that was put out, she returned and stuffed something in between two slices of bread for herself. Taking it outside with a glass of cold cola, she sat on the bench in the sunlight as she ate. Only when she had it in her mouth did she realise she'd chosen cheese and tomato.

She glanced across at the cat, who was tentatively washing it's ears. "This case is getting to me. I'll be a basket case by the time I'm finished." A massive sigh escaped her. "And I still don't know what I'm doing or whether I'm making any progress."

Still, she was mildly excited about catching Butterworth in a lie. It seemed unlikely she'd stumble over the killer so easily, especially since Butterworth was a bit young to fit Mrs Hunter's description, but it was something to pry at. She decided to go back to Henckle and Green to challenge him on the lie he'd told her. Then she realised he was her only current suspect. If he had an adequate explanation for the lie she'd be back at square one. She finished her lunch in a sombre mood and returned to her car.

It was about three thirty on that Friday afternoon when she got back to Henckle and Green and asked reception to call Phil Butterworth. This time she was asked to make her own way up and did so with a sense of determination. If this was going to be a pivotal interview in the case she was up to it.

The marketing suite seemed fairly empty and she wondered if it was usual for the staff to sneak out early on a Friday afternoon. Even Janice's desk had been tidy and cleared, suggesting she'd already left for the day. Only two people were in the main office. One was leant back, reading a newspaper, the other was Butterworth. He had his back to her and was busy filling boxes with possessions. That brought her up short.

"Oh," she said, all her pre-prepared attack forgotten. "Have you been sacked?"

She hadn't meant to ask the question so baldly, but he turned to look at her with gleaming eyes. "Oh no, I've got a new job. That is, I already had a new job, but I was working my notice. Eleanor called me in after lunch and said we can call it quits. Wilkins and Sons want me as soon as possible." He pulled a chair out for her and dropped into his own, showing a lot more confidence than he had previously. "Reception said you needed to talk to me again."

"I went over to the Stanford Street site," she began.

Once again, he went bright red in an instant. "That was a lie," he said before she could continue. "Well, not a lie, call it window-dressing. I did actually go there."

"Window-dressing?"

"I had the interview with Wilkins and Sons that morning. I didn't want anyone here knowing I was looking for another job, so I came up with an excuse for being in Nunsfield." He dropped his eyes. "I guess I should have told you the truth this morning, but everyone here had been told I was on site."

"I see," said Indigo, feeling a promising lead slipping away from her. "When was the interview? You couldn't have been there from nine until eleven, surely?"

He stood up, dug about in one of the boxes, pulled out a crumpled piece of paper and gave it to her. She glanced at it. It was from Wilkins and Sons on headed paper and invited Mr Philip Butterworth to an interview and psychometric test on Tuesday the 5th of August from 9:15 am.

"I got there at nine exactly," he said. "They did the test first, then the interview. I got out about ten forty five and went round to Stanford Street."

"Where do you live?" she asked.

"Nunsfield. This is a good job. It's not only better money and a better position, but it's right on my doorstep."

She wondered whether there was any point in asking him what he was doing between eight and nine? If it really had been the killer who drove Taylor's car into the Aldgate car park at nine twenty, then it looked like Butterworth had an alibi. A real one.

"I suppose the people at Wilkins and Sons would confirm you were there at nine that day?"

Panic entered the pale blue eyes. "Oh, give me a break! I haven't even started yet. You want to go and ask my new boss to alibi me for a murder?" He looked as if he was about to burst into tears.

She relented and shook her head. “Not unless it becomes absolutely necessary, but I do want to take this, if I may?” She waved the interview letter.

Butterworth nodded and straightened his shoulders. “Take it,” he said. “Look, I didn’t like Taylor. If you want my real opinion he was an uptight, prissy bore with no life outside work. But I didn’t kill him, I didn’t have any reason to kill him. I knew my career here was shot the moment Queen Bee started blaming me for under pricing the damned contract. Taylor’s attack was just salt in the wound. It hurt, but it didn’t make any real difference to my life.”

She studied his defiant expression and smiled to herself. With face and body both suffused with passion, he looked much more attractive and dynamic. If he could only channel some of that fervour into permanent confidence, he might just achieve that career he yearned for. Perhaps maturity and experience would do it for him.

She shook hands with him and wished him well in his new job.

On her way down in the lift, she mused on the very obvious ambitions of the people she’d come across in the past few days. Butterworth was a young man on the rise, despite a disastrous mistake which had almost stalled his career. Then there was Eleanor Knight with her power dressing and the certificates displayed on her wall. Young Janice had hopes that were likely to be disappointed. And what about that local government man, with his expensive suit and condescending air? Come to think of it, even Mike Nash saw himself as a champion of the natural world. As for Chief Inspector Waters, she’d begun to suspect his ambitions stretched all the way to Chief Constable.

Which led her thoughts to George Howard. George’s ambitions were more social than personal. To him, rank merely meant a better chance of removing the criminals who harmed other people. He hoped, one day, to be an SIO himself, but only so that he could direct investigations more effectively. He worked within the bureaucratic guidelines of PACE, but he was an old-fashioned copper at heart. She sighed. Which was why people like Waters would rise faster than him.

Thinking about the inspector gave her an idea of what to do next. She'd told Rupert she would widen her search to Taylor's friends and family, but to do that she needed to know who they were. The newspapers had been remarkably quiet on the subject, but Howard should have that information. Would he be willing to give it to her? Perhaps she should ask Rupert to contact him? No, if there was going to be an approach it had to come from her. She called him on his personal mobile number and explained her errand. He was wary and refused to discuss it over the phone, but agreed to meet her at a coffee shop in Nunsfield. It was a nuisance to have to make the seventeen mile drive to Oxely's second town twice in one day, but he was pursuing enquiries there and couldn't come to her.

Chapter Nine

The coffee shop was almost empty when she walked in, just a couple of female shoppers sitting at a table near the door, their bulging plastic bags spread over unused chairs. A few feet away a businessman was using the free wifi to check his emails as he swallowed a large latte and a sandwich. George was at a table towards the back of the long, narrow shop, hunched over his usual black Americano. Indigo waved and stopped at the counter to order a medium Cappuccino before joining him.

He waited until she was settled in the seat opposite before saying, "I can't give you the address of any witness, you know that."

She studied him and sipped at her coffee for a few moments. "I'm not asking for addresses," she said at last, "just names. And they're not witnesses, because there are no witness statements from them."

He looked troubled and ran his finger around the rim of his cup. "But you've been talking to people who have given statements."

She gave a sigh of pure irritation. "I'm allowed. You haven't even put a case together yet."

"I hope you haven't been trying to persuade them to change their testimony."

She gasped and felt the muscles in her jaw tauten. "Me persuading people to change their minds? Okay, you need to listen to this."

Taking her phone from her pocket, she selected the interview with Mrs Hunter and played it back. George listened with growing concern. When it finished, he sat for a moment in silence, then groaned. "Damn it, I knew Rick Waters was being single-minded on this case, but that's going too far." He met her eyes. "I'm glad you played me that. If she'd got up on the stand

and said what she told you, it would have knocked our case into Hell."

"You don't think it's there already?"

"It's based on very meagre circumstantial evidence, I grant you, and you've just knocked one of the legs from under it. But I don't have room for manoeuvre, Indie. The SIO determines the actions and we poor bloody troops do what we're told. I can't go off interviewing anyone I feel like." He pondered for a while, sipping at his coffee, then put the cup down and squared his shoulders. "But you can. Who else have you spoken to?"

"Nash, Amy and Abiola at the camp. They're the only ones left. And I went to Henckle and Green today and spoke with Eleanor Knight and Phil Butterworth."

"We didn't interview him. Did he say anything of interest?"

"He confirmed it was Amy who knocked Taylor down."

He nodded slowly. "Nash said the same thing. I'm afraid Amy was out of it when she was interviewed and she's been marked down as an unreliable witness."

"Look, George, all I want is to talk to Taylor's friends and family. You're obviously not interested in them, but I am."

"Why?"

"Because I have a feeling this murder wasn't about the desecration of the woods. I'm not saying it wasn't about the bypass, but I need to widen my search beyond the woods."

He laughed and, for a moment, she thought she saw affection in his eyes. Then he swallowed the final quarter cup of coffee in one gulp, took a deep breath, and shook his head. "Peter Taylor had no living family, and no close friends that we could trace either."

"He had a dog," she said. "What happened to that?"

"Yes, he had a Jack Russell called Abercrombie."

"Abercrombie?"

His eyebrows rose in a way he had when they were sharing a joke. "Named after Sir Patrick Abercrombie, one of Taylor's heroes. The dog was left with his downstairs neighbour when he was working away from home, and she's offered to keep it rather than let it go to strangers. I'll give you the address, but it's up to Mrs Barnes if she'll speak to you. She has the key to Taylor's flat. If you want to know something about him, try to get a look at that. It's very informative." He wagged the forefinger of his right hand in her direction. "But don't tell anyone I said that because I'll deny it."

She wrote down the address he dictated, gave him her sweetest smile in thanks, and watched silently as he rose and walked slowly down the shop towards the exit. Once he'd left, she lowered her head and stared into the fading froth of her coffee, feeling an indefinable sadness. She missed him, but did he miss her, or was he unconcerned about the breakdown of their budding romance?

She finished her coffee and glanced at the clock over the counter. It was after five. The address Howard had given her was in Surrey - Redhill. She was torn. It was too late to drive all the way over there now, but tomorrow was Saturday. She didn't really want to wait until Monday before speaking to Mrs Barnes. She decided to risk calling on the neighbour the following morning. She went back to the car and set off for home. Maisie would lock up the agency and there was nothing she needed to speak to either her or Rupert about that couldn't wait. Violet's name popped into her head, evoking feelings of guilt. She promised herself she'd call and update her sister as soon as she got back to the cabin.

Both Mike Nash and Phil Butterworth had given the impression Peter K. Taylor was all about concrete and steel and gleaming glass, so she'd expected his flat to be in some ultramodern block of futuristic design. She was puzzled, therefore, to find herself pulling up outside a very nice three story Georgian town house. It was all red brick and tall, white-painted windows. There were even tubs, hanging baskets and window boxes full of flowers adorning the outside. She rechecked the address in case she'd got it wrong, but no, this was the place alright. She looked back and realised the greenery didn't extend to the top floor, where Taylor had lived.

The grey front door held a discreet wooden plate naming the residents – Flat 1: D. Barnes; Flat 2: G. Fitzgerald; Flat 3: P. K. Taylor. She pushed the door and found it unlocked, opening into a tiny lobby, the hall of the original house before it had been subdivided into flats. Directly in front of her a staircase led up to flats 2 and 3. The door to flat 1 was to her right. She knocked.

The door was opened by a short, slight woman in her forties who studied her with suspicion. "Yes?" she said, in a tone so frosty it could have etched glass.

"Mrs Barnes? My name's Indigo Lattimer. I'm a private investigator and I've been hired to get background for the defence in the Peter K. Taylor murder. I wonder if you would answer —"

In the course of her career Indigo had had doors slammed in her face on numerous occasions and had learnt how to prevent them closing. This time she simply caught the door with her hand and stiffened her arm. She judged, rightly, that she was stronger than the woman pushing against her.

"Please, Mrs Barnes, at least hear me out."

"I'm not helping Peter's killer. I don't know how you have the gall to come round here and ask me to." She gave another shove, which Indigo easily resisted.

"What if Alan Sherman didn't kill Peter Taylor?" she suggested. "What if the police have the wrong man? Don't you want to be sure? You wouldn't want the wrong man to go to jail."

The pressure eased slightly, but Mrs Barnes said, "I'll let the jury decide that."

"Alright, if you don't want to talk to me, that's fine. But Inspector Howard suggested I look round Mr Taylor's flat. At least let me have the key so I can do so." She hadn't meant to use George's name and prayed the woman wouldn't try to either check or complain.

Mrs Barnes, however, took her words at face value. She stopped trying to close the door and the top half of her body appeared around it. "Well, I don't know what you expect to find looking around Peter's flat. The police searched it thoroughly." She looked Indigo over and stood for a moment with her lips pursed. "I don't trust you up there alone. I'll get the key and come with you."

Indigo allowed her to pull the door closed, wondering if her acquiescence was just a ploy. It seemed not, for in a few moments she was back with a set of keys in her hand. A small Jack Russell Terrier poked its head between her legs and she shooed it back inside and closed the door.

"Come on then," she said, starting up the carpeted stairs.

Indigo followed obediently, accepting that she wasn't going to get into the woman's flat to interview her properly. She decided to do the best she could while she was being shown around. Reaching inside her pocket, she took out her phone, switched it to record mode and held it discreetly by her side. "You referred to Mr Taylor as Peter. Was he a friend of yours?"

The thin back hunched in disapproval. "You sound surprised. People think he was antisocial, but he wasn't. He was a quiet man, accepted, but he had a very dry sense of humour."

They'd reached the first landing and the woman paused to catch her breath.

"You probably had to know him quite well to realise that," said Indigo. "The people he worked with described him as disappointed."

Mrs Barnes got moving again. "Ah, well," she said over her shoulder, "he had reason. Life wasn't kind to him."

She stopped at the door to the top flat and turned the key in the lock. Throwing the door open, she stepped aside to allow Indigo to go ahead, but followed her in. That suited Indigo perfectly. While Mrs Barnes was watching her to make sure she didn't steal the silver, she wouldn't be concentrating on her own verbal responses.

The door opened directly into the living room. Indigo looked around and immediately saw what George had meant. The room was scrupulously neat. The bookshelves contained ranks of books, all filed by height and carefully aligned. Each piece of furniture was arranged in precise relation to the other. This man wasn't just detailed, he was verging on OCD. She walked over to a bookcase and started examining the books. Town Planning, Architecture, they were almost all to do with the built environment. Taylor's work was also his passion. Mrs Barnes was hovering at her shoulder.

"So what did life do to him?" asked Indigo, deciding there'd been enough of a pause.

That startled the other woman. She stepped back a pace. "What didn't it do to him? He was engaged, you know, when he was a young man. She was a librarian."

"Sounds very suitable," murmured Indigo. "I take it the marriage didn't go ahead?"

"No. The girl got cold feet and ran off to California. Next thing Peter knew, she'd become an artist and married some layabout who wanted to act. It knocked the poor man for six, I can tell you."

Indigo was rifling through the neat rows of books. The nearest thing she could find to fiction was a group of biographies, all relating to architects and planners. She pulled out one on Patrick Abercrombie and read the blurb, discovering he'd been influential in the rebuilding of London after the Second World War. She looked at a couple of others and realised they were men who'd had the power to create whole environments. She began to understand the way Taylor's career had channelled his needs for order, power and creativity.

"You've known him since he was young, then?" she asked, realising she'd allowed the woman to stop talking again.

Mrs Barnes coughed delicately. "He came to live here about eight years ago, but he sometimes spoke about his fiancée. What she did confused him. I think it rather put him off women. He put all his energies into his work after that."

It began to look as if Mrs Barnes carried a bit of a torch for Peter Taylor. But something was worrying her about the flat. There was something missing. What could it be? "He told you that?" she asked, just to keep the conversation going.

"Why, yes. He often said he was married to his work and that was all he needed."

Sounded like Taylor was keeping the woman at bay. Ah, she had it. She turned and looked straight at the other woman. "Did the police take away his computer?"

"He didn't have one. Didn't like them."

"He must have had to use one at work."

"Just because he didn't like them, didn't mean he couldn't use one. I think he preferred doing things with his hands. He had very neat handwriting and his drawings are exceptional." She waved towards the walls.

Indigo had barely glanced at the framed drawings on the living room walls, thinking them merely pieces acquired for decoration. Now that she looked more closely she could see the beautifully observed sketches were all by the same hand. Each had a neat signature in the bottom right hand corner. They were all pictures of buildings, and many of them were old buildings, confirming Taylor's love of architectural perfection hadn't been confined to concrete and steel.

"These are really good," she said, turning to face the hovering neighbour.

The woman's expression became slightly wistful. "They are, aren't they? I wanted him to sketch me, but he said he didn't do portraits."

"I see." Indigo made her way out of the living room into a tiny hall and on towards the single bedroom. On the way she stopped briefly to glance around the frighteningly clean and tidy kitchen and bathroom. Mrs Barnes padded along behind her. Before Indigo could formulate another question, the woman returned to her earlier statement, suggesting she'd been brooding on the subject.

"Yes, he was married to his job," she repeated. "That's why it's such a shame what happened."

Indigo tensed. Good, she was beginning to get proper information now. "And what did happen?" she asked in a casual tone as she entered the bedroom and began to search through drawers.

"He was made redundant. You must know that. The people he worked with for all those years just tossed him on the scrap heap." There was heavy indignation in her voice and Indigo thought it possible she was unconsciously mimicking the tone Taylor had used.

"Mind you," Mrs Barnes continued in a more confiding voice, "they'd had it in for him for years. I don't think they ever did really appreciate him. After he won all those awards for them as well. But there, he wasn't the kind to make up to the bosses, if you know what I mean." She made a great play of pushing in a drawer that Indigo had left slightly open. "Then, of course, he had some silly spat with a young man who did make up to the bosses and Peter was the one to suffer."

Indigo stopped turning over neatly folded shirts and underwear and stood up straight. "How did he suffer?"

"His career stalled, didn't it?" She paused and frowned. "Apparently the young man had connections among the senior managers and the row put paid to any more promotions for poor Peter. Then they made him redundant. He reckoned that was part of his punishment."

For a moment Indigo thought she might be onto something. "When did this spat take place?"

"Five or six years ago." Mrs Barnes gave an embarrassed little laugh. "I did tell him it wasn't likely the two things were connected, what with the redundancy coming after the young man had left the place. Still," she straightened her shoulders and met Indigo's eyes defiantly, "he was an unfortunate man. Nothing ever quite worked out for him. Now, have you finished?"

Indigo nodded and closed the drawer she'd been examining. Nothing in the flat had been of any use to her, and the incidents Mrs Barnes had related were ancient history. All she'd done was paint a picture of an obsessive man with severe problems relating to other people. She shivered at the cold emptiness of the place and turned towards her guide.

Mrs Barnes was leading her out of the flat and she followed, taking a last look around her as she walked. There was something sad about the place. Sad, but definitely not cheap.

"He was working as a consultant," she said as they started back down the stairs. "Why didn't he just retire? Surely he didn't need the money?"

"Oh no, it wasn't that. He had his council pension and a good redundancy package, and he made quite a bit a few years back when his mother died and he sold her house. That's when he moved in here." She waved her hand in a vague arc. "No." She stopped and turned to give Indigo a reproving look. "He was married to his work. I told you. He was passionate about planning and building. Creating order out of chaos, he used to call it. He didn't have anything else apart from Abercrombie."

She gave a deep sigh that might have been either frustration or resignation, and started down the rest of the stairs. “Poor Peter, he didn’t deserve to die like that. It was just his bad luck.”

Chapter Ten

Sunday was a quiet day. There was no one else she could think of to interview and she spent the morning pottering in her garden. When she'd converted the station into a home, the space between the platforms had seemed ideal for a sunken garden and had originally held raised vegetable beds, fruit bushes and miniature fruit trees. But long periods away from home had caused havoc to her planting and she'd eventually turned it into a paved patio surrounded by easy-care bushes. Today, she wandered around pulling out weeds and dead-heading rose bushes. Trying to occupy herself, of course, but nothing was working. It was occupying her hands, but not her mind, and that mind was contemplating the murder victim.

The pristine, but soulless, flat and the narrative by Mrs Barnes had presented a totally different picture of Taylor to the one she'd initially built up. She'd seen him as a difficult man who didn't like people and was prone to provoking them. She'd even begun to wonder if he was always destined to be a victim of murder. Now she realised he was just a lonely man with over-exacting standards. Did he hold himself to those standards? Probably. Maybe he was an only child, who hadn't been properly socialised. Maybe he did have OCD and found chaos difficult to handle. The woods would have represented chaos, with their unruly plants and meandering paths.

She stopped, with a dandelion still in one gloved hand. How desperate he must have been for company to have allowed an animal into his life. She glanced across at Midnight, sleeping flat out on a stone bench, ears twitching in catly dreams, and smiled. She could understand the companionship a pet gave to someone who lived alone. She'd never had a pet before, they didn't fit in with her father's regimented lifestyle.

When Midnight had stumbled onto her house platform, it had proved beneficial to both of them.

George had said — An ice-sharp dart pierced her gut. He'd be at home now. Perhaps it was his week to have the girls, she couldn't remember. Maisie too would be at home, cheerily preparing a midday meal for her husband and sons. Even the guesthouse across on the other platform was empty, Rupert having gone to visit his parents. But it was George Howard who had left the chasm in the pit of her stomach.

"Damn it!" She dropped her trowel and jumped to her feet. It was impossible to go on like this. If their nascent romance was truly over, then she'd have to find some way to get him out of her system.

Midnight had raised her head at the interruption and was giving her an indignant look. She laughed. "Go back to sleep. I'm going for a walk. Don't wait up." Perhaps a long walk by the river would give her some perspective, both on the case, and on her love life. She climbed the steps up towards the house.

Indigo got into the office early on Monday and added Phil Butterworth's name to the suspect list just to be thorough. Yet the truth was she still had no viable suspects apart from Alan. Her Sunday walk had produced no new insights. She stared at the board for a while, willing something to jump out at her, but nothing did. By the time Maisie arrived she was even beginning to sympathise with DCI Waters. What was not to like about Alan Sherman as a suspect when there were so few alternatives? Except, of course, that he no longer fitted the description provided by the only eye witness.

A head of red hair peered round the door and asked, "Would you like a coffee, pet?"

She nodded without turning round. “Make it strong, will you? I need the caffeine to kick-start my brain.”

Maisie entered the room and stood behind her. “That bad?”

Indigo swivelled in her chair and looked up at her. “I don’t have any suspects. I don’t know what the motive was. And I don’t know where to look next. I don’t think it could be any worse.”

“Didn’t anything come up with the friends and family?” asked Rupert, coming into the room and dropping into the chair beside her.

“There aren’t any. Just a neighbour who seems to have been key holder, dog minder and sole confidante.”

“There you are then,” said Maisie, disappearing in the direction of the kitchen, “she’ll know everything.”

“If she does,” muttered Indigo, “she isn’t telling it to me. All I could get out of her was what a miserable life Taylor had had.”

Rupert bounced to his feet and put his arms around his employer in a hug. “Hey boss, don’t give up. You’ll find something.”

She patted his arm and gave an appreciative chuckle. “I’m not giving up,” she promised. “It’s just that I don’t know how to approach a murder case. I wonder what the police would do?”

He straightened up and studied her, head on one side as he thought. “Well, they start by combing the crime scene. You could go over the forensic reports again.”

“But it wasn’t the crime scene, was it? Just the place where the body was —” She stopped and shook herself. “That’s an idea, you know. How would you like to go and see where Taylor’s body was found?”

“Great!” He plonked back down in his chair and crossed his arms, watching her intently. “There won’t be any evidence left, though. I bet those Scene of Crime boys are pretty thorough."

"I wasn't really thinking of physical evidence. Although," she hesitated, "it wouldn't do any harm to check, just in case they missed something. No, I just wondered if seeing the site where Taylor was dumped would give us some psychological insight into the killer."

"I'm with you there," said Maisie, coming in with a tray of steaming mugs. "You can learn a lot about a bloke by where he leaves his cast-offs." She dumped the tray on the table in front of the couple. "Rod drops his dirty clothes in a pile behind the bedroom chair. I reckon it shows a secretive nature."

Indigo laughed and took her mug from the tray. "It shows he's frightened of you. Why don't you put a linen basket behind the chair for him?"

Maisie raised her brows in mock horror. "What, and take away his one source of rebellion?" She gave a broad wink. "He has to have some outlet for the messy side of his personality. I have the rest of the house organised like an army camp."

Indigo was still chuckling to herself at the thought of Maisie organising her men folk like army recruits as she and Rupert drove out to the scene. By the time they left the car and began to trudge along the edge of the path looking for the dump site, a wind had blown up. The trees were whipping and swaying around them, shedding barely brown leaves in piles. It made them look like they were shaking their heads in protest, attempting to turn herself and Rupert away. Recalling the struggle of her earlier visit to the area, she had the strangest feeling they were determined to preserve their secrets at all cost.

"Why not," she muttered under her breath, "everyone else is."

They had a sketch map of the dump site and copies of the scene-of-crime photos, but things change in a month and the windy conditions were disturbing the scene even more. She was finding it extremely difficult to reconcile the photographs with the plants actually lining the path and finally stopped in frustration, scanning the area around her desperately.

"I don't think we're even going to find the site," said Rupert, his initial enthusiasm plummeting, as it sometimes did.

But she'd just seen a tattered length of black and yellow plastic tape tied to a tree, streaming like a windsock in the prevailing wind. It was further off the path than she'd expected from Alan's description, making her realise the body dump hadn't been quite as blatant has she'd thought. She tapped Rupert on the shoulder and pointed. "Here we are."

At her insistence they donned latex gloves and plastic shoe covers before venturing into the area where Taylor's body had been left. Rupert, whose one flaw as an investigator was impatience with procedure, gave an exaggerated sigh. "Even if we find anything, we can't be sure it wasn't dropped since the police were here."

She was surveying the area, matching the scene against the photographs. "Never mind," she soothed absently, "we're not looking for physical evidence, remember?" She turned towards him. "Do you see anything odd about where the body was found?"

He looked at the plant she was indicating, not really a bush, more a patch of greenery that looked like it had flowered earlier in the year. "What is that?" he asked.

"Wood Sorrel, I think. It doesn't give very good cover and it's quite visible from the path." She pointed back to the hard packed dirt track they'd walked along. "I can understand Taylor being left this close to the road. After all, a dead body's really difficult for one person to move, and the killer wouldn't want to leave the car for too long. But why shove it under a patch of flowers just a few feet from a path? A little bit further in and it wouldn't have been seen at all." She waved towards an area of denser planting some three feet away. " Alan said one foot was sticking out, which was careless in the extreme."

"Then you were right, boss. The killer wanted the body found."

"Exactly. And he wanted it found here. This path goes right past the protest camp." She glanced around her as she thought it through. "I don't think he wanted it found by the protestors, though. He did make some attempt at concealment. I think he was hoping for a passer-by. A dog walker, maybe."

Rupert blinked and gave her a puzzled look. "What makes you think he didn't want one of the protestors to find it?"

"I don't know. Just instinct. If Mike Nash had found the body, he'd probably have moved it away from the camp." She bent and started idly pushing the Sorrel leaves aside, scanning the ground for anything that might still be there. "Our killer wanted to frame the protestors, so it would suit him better for the body to be found by an innocent member of the public."

Rupert didn't answer. He'd started rummaging through the greenery himself, like an eager child searching for Easter eggs. She shook her head, reminding herself he was still young and had plenty of time to learn to curb his enthusiastic nature. She concentrated on her own patch of ground, but it was remarkably clean after being forensically examined. A few minutes later, however, she called her assistant over and asked, "What do you make of this?"

He followed her pointing finger. "What? I can't see anything."

"This scattering of gravel."

He peered closer, his eyebrows knitting as he tried to guess her reasoning. "It's just gravel, you find it all over the place."

"But not in these woods. Look around you, Rupert. The ground surface is earth, leaf mould, organic matter. None of the paths are gravelled, they're all just compacted earth."

"The little lay-by further up the road has gravel just like this," he argued. "It probably came from there."

"How? There's too much of it to have been carried on a shoe, and it's underneath the Sorrel plant." She watched his face as he thought her question over. She could see he hadn't yet caught up with the possibility running around her mind, and decided to put him out of his misery. "You remember how Waters thought Alan's bracelet had fallen into the plastic sheeting and landed on the body as it was rolled free?" He nodded. "What if Taylor was killed on gravel like this, and some of it got caught up in the plastic as it was wrapped?"

He grimaced, obviously finding her conclusion less stunning than she'd hoped. "What if he was? That's pretty common gravel. It could have come from anywhere."

That deflated her, reminding her yet again of the difficult nature of this case. "Yes, I suppose it could." She stood silently contemplating the handful of gravel for a few minutes, wondering if her investigation had finally reached a dead end. Perhaps George had been right and she wasn't cut out for criminal work. "We could look at that lay-by," she sighed, "just to be thorough. Although it seems strange someone would move a body just a few hundred yards. Why go to all that trouble?"

"To point the finger at the protestors!" Rupert bounced back to his normal cheerful self, as if she'd presented him with a major clue. "He couldn't ask Taylor to meet him on the path to the protest camp, could he? That would be stupid. But if they met at the lay-by he wouldn't have so far to carry the body to where he wanted it."

Indigo was doubtful. It seemed a very elaborate plan somehow, but there were definite hints of a plan of some kind in this murder. The killer had brought plastic sheeting with him to minimise blood transfer, and that axe wasn't something people carried around with them in the normal course of things. Had the killer known about the axe at the protest camp? She shook herself, worried she was letting her fancy run away with her. "I suppose you could arrange to meet someone at a lay-by, especially if your victim was coming by car." She pulled the greenery further away from the ground and said, "Take some pictures of this, will you. Then I think we will take a look at that lay-by. I'd kick myself if we didn't and it turned out to be important."

Rupert pulled a small digital camera out of his pocket and did as he was told. Once she was happy he'd adequately recorded the scene, she allowed the plant to settle gently back into place and the pair walked back to the path before removing their shoe coverings and gloves.

They left the car where it was and fought their way to the lay-by along the verge, stepping around nettles and large clumps of tough grass. "You could lose just about anything amongst this stuff," said Indigo in disgust.

The lay-by was really just a large bite out of the verge, barely big enough for two cars to pull in nose-to-tail. Its real function was to enable cars to pull over and allow larger vehicles to pass on the narrow road, but it made a convenient place to get the car off the road if you wanted to visit the woods. It was probably used a lot by dog-walkers and a signpost at one end of it told motorists they could only park for an hour. She thought that was probably ignored, since traffic wardens weren't going to be patrolling this remote stretch of road. As Rupert had said, the area was surfaced with a thick layer of gravel rather than tarmac.

Indigo wondered briefly why she hadn't parked here rather than risking the underside of her car on the verge near the dump site, then remembered the difficult trek they'd just made. "I'd have driven the body that few yards as well," she muttered. "I wouldn't want to drag anything heavy through all this undergrowth."

Rupert glanced back along the length of verge and then up and down the road. "No, it'd take quite a while. You wouldn't want to be seen, would you?" He scratched his curly head and pulled a face. "There's only been one car, though, all the time we've been walking."

"I noticed. It's not an impossible place to commit murder if you were organised. Let's put the gloves and shoe covers back on, just in case. If we find anything we'll have to call the police in and we don't want to contaminate the scene."

She trod carefully onto the gravel surface and began a thorough visual search. Rupert remained on the verge and began rifling through the weeds that edged the lay-by. They must have been searching for about fifteen minutes before Indigo spotted a suspicious patch of crusty black material under the gravel close to the verge and Rupert simultaneously said, "Look what I've found."

She looked up. He was only a couple of feet away from her, almost within touching distance. He'd pushed a patch of grass aside to reveal a small white object. As she turned her head, he was just about to reach down and pick it up.

"Don't," she ordered. "It may be important. We need to record it before we do anything else."

"It's an iPhone."

"I can see that." She stepped carefully onto the verge near Rupert and took over his hold on the grass. "Get out your camera. I want it photographed from every possible angle."

"Aren't we going to look at it?" He sounded disappointed, but took the camera from his pocket as directed.

"Of course we are, we need to check the contents. For all we know it could belong to a careless dog-walker. I'm not calling Inspector Howard out on a wild goose chase." But her heart was racing. Peter Taylor had owned an iPhone for his work, and it hadn't been found. Not on his body, not in the car, not back in the office at H&G. Maybe it had been lying here on the edge of the woods for the last four weeks.

Once Rupert had taken enough photos to satisfy even the most scrupulous of forensic scientists, Indigo picked up four pieces of gravel and used them to mark the exact position of the phone on the ground. Only then did she gingerly raise it high enough to see the screen, which was worryingly blank. She wondered whether it would still function after a month exposed to the elements. Anything from rain seepage to a flat battery could mean there would be no response when she pushed the buttons. She began by trying to switch it on, and was rewarded by seeing it flicker into life.

Unfortunately, the screen was now asking for a password. She swore under her breath, causing Rupert to blink and say "Boss?" She shook her head, wondering what the uptight Taylor would use as a password. Something to do with architecture, probably. Then inspiration struck and she typed in the name Abercrombie. To her relief, the lock page gave way to a screen full of apps.

She clicked to the emails and saw straight away that the phone did indeed belong to Taylor. She wondered why it had been switched off. Was his last meeting so private he didn't want to be disturbed? This might be an ideal place for the killer, but it was a very strange place for Taylor to agree to meet someone. Unless, of course, said an annoying little voice in her head, he was meeting one of the protestors. But then, why move the body closer to the camp?

Growling with frustration, she brought up the Call Log and told Rupert to write down the numbers as she read them out. There weren't a lot of them. During the whole of the two months he'd been working for Henckle and Green he'd only had telephone contact with nine other people. Once all the numbers were safely recorded, she turned the iPhone off and gently replaced it within the frame of stones she'd laid down.

Placing the four stones back onto the gravel surface, she released the grass and stood up.

"Go back to the office and check on those numbers. I want to know everyone Taylor was in contact with since he got to Great Oxing." As he put the notepad in his pocket she reached out her hand. "Oh, and give me the memory chip out of the camera. I'll have to turn it over to the police."

"If I take the car, how will you get back?"

"Don't worry about that, it's only half a mile to the nearest bus stop. It won't kill me."

Chapter Eleven

George's response to her call was gratifyingly positive. He asked her to remain where she was and promised to be there with a full forensics team as soon as practically possible. He was as good as his word, and a small fleet of cars drew up along the little road just under fifty minutes later. The first contained George himself and a uniformed constable.

"No DCI Waters?" she queried as he walked towards her.

"He'll come out if necessary, Miss," he said in full official mode. "Let's see what we've got first."

"As I told you Inspector, it's Taylor's iPhone." She realised he wanted to keep things formal around his colleagues and was happy to play along, not quite sure in her own mind how to relate to him in these circumstances. "I think this may be where he was killed. Not so far from the dump site, after all. It looks like there's blood on some of the gravel and soaked into the ground underneath."

He glanced sideways at her, his eyes narrowing in concern. "Have you been clumping around my crime scene, contaminating the evidence?"

"For pity's sake!" Her exasperation made her forget formality. "Give me some credit. We wore gloves and shoe covers. I've photographs of both the gravel and the phone in situ, and I put the phone back exactly where it was after I checked it."

He raised his hands, palms out. "Okay, okay, but even I get into trouble with the SOCO boys for stepping in the wrong place or moving the wrong thing." He took a deep breath and said quietly, "Did you have to touch the phone?"

"Yes," she said, forcing herself to calm, "of course I did. Until I checked it, I had no way of knowing who the owner was.

You wouldn't have liked me getting the whole band of you out here for nothing."

He ran the fingers of his right hand through his thick locks as he considered her words. "I'll concede the point," he said at last. "It's not easy to identify someone else's phone just by looking at it."

She held out the memory chip from the camera. "Here are our crime scene photos. I don't have duplicates, so I'd appreciate getting it back once your people have uploaded them."

He took the chip from her hand, his fingers brushing awkwardly against hers. "I'll do my best." He looked around, his eyes scanning the road. "I don't see your car. How did you get here?"

"I came with Rupert. He had to go back to the office." She saw his eyes narrow ever so slightly and knew he was suspicious. That was the trouble with him knowing her so well. "Don't worry," she said quickly, trying to divert his thoughts, "I can get a bus back into town."

"Nonsense, PC Ross will drive you back." He indicated his own car and the uniformed officer standing behind him. "Just show the team where everything is, then you can go." The three cars parked raggedly behind his had disgorged a small team of white-suited technicians who stood chattering on the grass verge. He bobbed his head briefly in their direction, then turned back to face her. "I'll need a statement later, you understand that?"

She nodded and took a step towards the group, but he caught hold of her upper arm and leant close to her ear. "Be careful if you're going to check the numbers from the phone log. You could be dealing with a very dangerous individual."

She turned her head and looked him straight in the eyes, seeing concern in their brown depths. "Don't worry," she murmured, "I can defend myself. You know that."

"Of course I worry. Damn it, Indie —"

She hesitated, but this was no place for a private conversation. She gave him a rueful smile and changed the subject. "The password is 'Abercrombie' by the way."

He released her reluctantly and she continued towards the waiting scientists. When she returned to claim her ride he was still standing at the edge of the road watching her. His strained expression caused her a twinge of guilt. His words had suggested two things to her. First, he was beginning to have doubts about Alan's guilt. Second, he really did care about her.

"Let's hope they're both true," she breathed, causing PC Ross to give her a puzzled look.

She was in something of an exultant mood when she got back to the agency, but was soon brought back to earth by the sight of Maisie and Rupert huddled in the outer office in front of the large beige sofa she'd installed for the benefit of those clients who arrived early for their appointment. Perched on the edge of the sofa was Violet, her small frame dwarfed by the six foot long seat. She was crying raggedly and Maisie was patting her with her right hand and offering a glass of water with her left.

"What's wrong?" Indigo demanded expecting the worst, whatever form that might take.

"Alan's been attacked," blurted Rupert before anyone else could speak.

Maisie frowned at him and added quickly, "It's just cuts and bruises. No real harm done."

Violet's weeping increased in volume and Indigo frowned at her personal assistant. This was no time for that cool practicality. She slid onto the sofa beside her sister and put an arm around her shoulder, making a shooing motion to the other two. "What happened?" she asked gently as her staff obeyed her instruction and left them alone.

Violet rubbed at her damp eyes and looked up at her. "Alan's cellmate didn't like his accent." She shook her head as if nothing made sense any more. "I don't know, Indie. He beat up my baby because he was a posh boy, that's what Tony Dawson told me. Alan's in the hospital wing tonight and they're going to put him in with someone less violent, but I'm scared. What's going to happen to him?"

Indigo made soothing noises and rocked her backwards and forwards. "It's going to be alright, Vi. I'll get him out, I promise I will. The thug who hurt him will be punished and they'll take better care of Alan now they know he can't defend himself." But that was a blatant lie. Word would soon get round the prison that Sherman was an easy target.

Her sister sniffed and straightened her shoulders. "That's nonsense, and you know it. I always know when you're lying." She pulled herself free of Indigo's arms and stood up. "I just wanted you to know what happened. I wanted you to see how urgent it was to get Alan out."

Indigo rose herself and took Violet by the shoulders. "I do see, Vi. I'm doing the best I can, but things aren't straightforward. If they were, he wouldn't have been arrested in the first place." She bent and brushed her sister's forehead with her lips. "I've told you I'll get him out, even if I have to hunt down the real killer. Whatever it takes."

Violet nodded, kissed her cheek, retrieved her handbag from the sofa and turned away. Indigo stood and watched her walk to the door and go through it, closing it behind her. She was troubled, recalling how she'd felt at a dead end before the trip to the woods. What if the discoveries in the lay-by yielded no further clues? What if she couldn't follow through on her promise to Violet?

Maisie, who knew her a lot better than she liked, slid silently into the room and said, "Don't go blaming yourself. There's nothing you could have done to prevent it. They shouldn't have put him in a cell with a young thug who's in for GBH."

Indigo turned to meet her eyes. "Alan's charged with a brutal murder. Maybe they thought he could take care of himself."

"Which just goes to show what morons they are." She gave a snort of disgust. "You're going to blame yourself, anyway. Aren't you?"

Indigo shook her head and fought against a tightening of her jaw. "I'm not doing Alan or Vi much good at present. None of my interviews have got me anywhere."

"Well, pet," said Maisie, ever practical, "you won't get him out of prison standing there, beating yourself up."

She took a deep breath and gave a determined nod "You're quite right." She noticed Rupert lurking in the corridor and turned in his direction. "And I have some new leads to follow up. Don't I?"

He came in and offered her his notebook. "I've identified all the phone numbers." He agreed, but sounded glum. "I don't know how much use they are. They all seem to be work related."

She took the notebook and ran her eyes down the list of numbers. They weren't all work related, three were personal. One number belonged to Mrs Barnes, one to Taylor's dentist, and the third to his accountant. Rupert had added a note that the accountant had been preparing Taylor's tax return. Of the rest, three were Henckle and Green numbers; Eleanor Knight, Phil Butterworth and Janice. The final three were of slightly more interest – Derian Winslow, Councillor Bill Porter, and Ronald Spencer-Cooper.

She turned to Rupert. "Isn't Spencer-Cooper the owner of the Country Club? I remember Eleanor Knight mentioning the name."

"That's right. He wasn't in when I phoned. The number was diverted to the Course Manager, a Barry Raven."

"Mm, why would Taylor be calling Ronald Spencer-Cooper? Surely we haven't got this murder upside down?"

"What do you mean, pet?" demanded Maisie. "How could it be upside down?"

"Well, we've been following the police lead, assuming it had something to do with the bypass destroying the woods."

"The body was found in the woods," put in Rupert quickly. "It's natural to assume they had something to do with the death."

She gave him an old-fashioned look. "But we know the dump site was a deliberate misdirection. Don't forget the road was originally meant to go through Country Club land and Taylor was doing his best to get it returned to that route in order to save H&G money."

"Wow," said Rupert, "I hadn't thought of that. Didn't you say Spencer-Cooper would have lost his appeal?"

"Eleanor Knight thought so. I wonder how important it is to him to avoid losing that piece of land." She stood up and handed the notebook to Maisie. "See if you can get me appointments with Spencer-Cooper, Councillor Porter, and Winslow. I want to find out exactly what Taylor's thoughts were about that change of route." She turned and began walking towards her office.

Maisie called after her. "What are you going to be doing?"

"I'm going to review that interview with Eleanor Knight and see exactly what she did say about Spencer-Cooper's appeal. If you can get any of those appointments for today, I'd be grateful."

Chapter Twelve

Great Oxing Golf and Country Club had begun life as a single golf course with a shed of a club house and a rough tarmac car park. Over the years Ronald Spencer-Cooper had built it up, little by little, into a smart and exclusive establishment which attracted the rich, the famous and the powerful. Although it was largely the quality of the second golf course, known as the B course, which had made it so popular, its success was also helped by a small five star hotel, complete with spa, gym and award-winning restaurant.

Indigo had been intrigued to discover it was the B course that had been threatened by the original bypass route, prompting some celebrities to write letters of protest to the council. It seemed the course rated with the best in the country, and had hosted its own well-attended golf tournament for the past three years.

As well as the hotel building there was a members-only club house, and this was where Spencer-Cooper kept his office. She arrived with forty minutes to spare before her meeting, having left the agency as soon as Maisie said Spencer-Cooper would see her. She parked in the visitor's car park and entered the double glass doors of the club house, finding herself in a lobby where several notice boards displayed lists of winners, club rules and regulations, notices of forthcoming events, and other information of interest to members. The right-hand wall contained a door to the men's toilets. She went through the single door opposite the main entrance and found herself in the bar area.

It was two thirty and the tables and stools were empty, the members having all returned to the courses for their afternoon games. Only the bar steward was visible, washing and drying glasses behind the bar. Perhaps she could pump him for information on Spencer-Cooper. She went over and gave him one of her most persuasive smiles.

"Look, I'm a bit early for a meeting with Mr Spencer-Cooper and I haven't had any lunch," she told him. "Is there any chance of a coffee and a sandwich?"

He looked up and frowned at her. "It's members only, madam. I'm not allowed to serve outsiders."

"But I am here to see the proprietor. Surely that makes me his guest, after a fashion?"

She could see him turning her argument over in his mind, then he shrugged. "Since the cook's still here, I'll see what I can do."

"Thanks. I'll take whatever's easiest."

He stuck his head through the door behind the counter and had a brief conversation with someone inside the kitchen, then returned to tell her there was some chicken left. She agreed to a chicken sandwich and he called the order over his shoulder. "That'll be six pound thirty five," he told her, ringing up the sale. "Are you here for a job?"

"Actually," she said, handing over money for her lunch order, "I'm working on the Peter K. Taylor murder."

"You're a police officer?" he asked as he dropped the money into the till.

"A private investigator."

He accepted that without comment and returned to washing and drying glasses. After a brief silence, he said, "I'm not surprised he got himself killed. He wasn't a nice man."

So, he was one of the slow, thoughtful types? "Oh, you knew him then? I didn't think he was a golfer."

He looked up, his eyes narrowing . "He wasn't, but he came to talk to the governor once."

"Mr Spencer-Cooper?"

"That's what I said."

She allowed a suitable pause, but he wasn't going to elaborate. "What made you think he wasn't nice?"

Her order arrived and he took it from the cook and placed it on the bar top in front of her. She wondered if he would answer her question, and took a bite out of the sandwich as she waited. It seemed he'd been considering the matter from all angles, because he eventually spoke. "He made the governor angry. It's not like Mr Spencer-Cooper to get angry. He's a very easy going man, but he got angry that day. I could hear the two of them from right out here."

She swallowed the chunk of food and asked, as casually as she could manage, "I wonder what they were arguing about?"

"I couldn't say." He finished the last glass, emptied the bowl, put it into a cupboard under the counter, then met her eye. "Even if I'd heard the words, I wouldn't go telling the governor's business to a complete stranger."

"Quite right." She smiled encouragingly. "I like loyalty in a man."

He snorted and walked away, retreating through the door into the kitchen to join the cook. Realising that was all she was going to get, Indigo picked up her plate and cup and moved to a table to complete her meal.

At five past three a stocky man of medium height entered the bar and looked round. He had blue eyes and very short, light brown hair. She quickly guessed he kept it so short to hide the fact it was getting thin. He came across to her. "Miss Lattimer?" he asked pleasantly, though his eyes wouldn't quite meet hers.

She stood up and shook the hand he was offering, then followed him down the corridor to his office. In contrast to Eleanor Knight's room, this one practically blasted her with it's owner's personality. There were two sets of golf clubs in the corner, golf trophies on desk and filing cabinet, various pictures on the walls showing him with people in golfing gear, some of them celebrities. Good heavens, was that Tiger Woods? On his desk, though, the photos were more personal. A woman of around his own age, two teenage girls, and a teenage boy. Wife and children, she thought.

He pulled forward a seat for her, removing a pile of golf magazines, but still avoided proper eye contact. He was practically reeking edginess as he settled into his chair, using the desk as a shield between them. Why was she having this effect on people? Perhaps it was the nature of the crime. There was something unsettling about the brutality of a murder. No wonder the police had problems getting to the truth in murder investigations.

She forced her attention back to Spencer-Cooper, who was saying, "I don't know what help I can be, Miss Lattimer. I didn't really know Mr Taylor."

"But he did come to see you," she said. "He had your number in his phone."

"He came once." His voice was low and wary. He picked up a small trophy from his desk and began turning it around in his hands like a worry ball.

"And the two of you quarrelled." Seeing the look in his eyes, she added, "violently."

"I ...." His voice squeaked and he tried again, more robustly. "I don't know where you heard that."

"You didn't quarrel?"

He squared his jaw. "We had a vigorous discussion."

"What about?"

"My dear madam, that's entirely my business."

He had cringed back, making it look like she had the upper hand in this conversation. Her voice became as smooth as ice cream. "Mr Spencer-Cooper, you met with Peter Taylor a few days before his murder and had a violent argument with him. If the subject of that argument was as innocent as you imply, why would you need to conceal it?"

He flinched and replaced the trophy on the desk. "If you must know, we talked about my appeal against the Compulsory Purchase Order for my land."

"Which was dropped."

"The order was dropped. The Council altered the route."

"That's what I meant." She leant back in her chair, contrasting her calmness with his lack of ease. "Why did he want to know about the appeal?"

"He wanted to know the grounds for my appeal. I told him it was based on loss of business."

"Would you lose much business? I understand the council were offering alternative land."

"God, you're as bad as he was. You can't just pick up the B course and stick it somewhere else. Even if you could totally recreate the greens and bunkers and everything else, which is impossible, you still wouldn't have the same course. It's the totality of the environment that makes a golf course great. Even something as small as wind direction and speed can make a difference to the way the ball flies."

There was real passion and despair in the speech. She leant forward, towards him. "And the B course is great, isn't it?" she said. "It's doubled your membership."

"It's trebled my membership and improved the class of member. That might sound snobbish, but it's the way things are. I've even had to impose membership conditions over the last five years."

"What sort of membership conditions?" she asked, intrigued by this glimpse into an alien environment.

The real interest in her tone caused him to straighten up and puff out his chest. "Well, I started by introducing a hefty joining fee, you know. That was to keep the numbers down, so the greens didn't get too crowded. Then I created a Members Committee to vet applicants. We'd begun to get a groupie element who only wanted to be close to the celebrity members.

I can't have my customers being pestered by over-zealous fans. They come here for relaxation, it's up to me to see they get it."

"I see." She thought it over. "And this is all because the B course is so good?"

"It's more than good, it's championship level. Almost up with St Andrews."

"So, losing the land to the bypass would have devastated your business?"

The wind went out of him and he collapsed back to his original state. "Yes. You have no idea what nightmares I had when I got that CPO."

"Did Taylor tell you he was hoping to reinstate the original route?"

"Oh, yes. Henckle and Green don't want the effort of digging up the woodland." His voice became bitter. "They'd rather plough through my greens instead."

"Is that what you argued about?"

"If you want to call it an argument," he said quietly, "then yes, it is."

He was lying. So, what could have been worse than Taylor wanting to tear up his precious greens? She paused, trying to frame a new question. Before she could formulate one, Spencer-Taylor started speaking again.

"You've got to understand, Taylor was a public sector type. He'd spent all his life in local government. He didn't appreciate how tenuous commercial success can be."

"He didn't understand the bottom line?"

"Precisely." He put his hands together in a prayer-like gesture. "Look, Miss Lattimer, I didn't like the man. He was too cold for my taste, too ... directed, but I didn't wish him any ill. I didn't think he could sway the Planning Committee anyway, so why would I want to harm him?"

She nodded absently. He was hiding something, but she was unlikely to get at it in this session. "Tell me," she asked, almost as an afterthought, "are Derian Winslow and Councillor Porter members of the club?"

To her surprise, that phased him more than anything else she'd asked. A look of panic crossed his features. "I ... I don't know. You'd have to ask the Membership Secretary. I don't know all the members, especially the local ones."

So, she should take that as a Yes, should she? Now why would mention of those two names spook him so much? He'd just been telling her how much he despised public sector types, so why did her question about two council officials make him so nervy?

Before she could ask anything more, he jumped to his feet and thrust a hand in her direction. "You'll have to excuse me now," he said. "I have another meeting I have to get to."

She allowed him to bundle her out of his office, figuring she'd got as much as she was going to anyway, and made her way thoughtfully out of the building, heading for the car park. She felt the interview had been interesting, and possibly fruitful. By the sound of it, Ronald Spencer-Cooper had a good deal more to gain from Taylor's death than anyone else she'd met so far.

"Miss Lattimer?" The voice was female and hesitant.

She looked up. A young woman was standing in front of her, her hands tucked into the back pockets of the ubiquitous jeans. Indigo recognised her from the photos on Spencer-Cooper's desk.

"You're Mr Spencer-Cooper's daughter, aren't you?"

The young woman nodded and released her hands in order to put one forward. "Lily," she said.

She shook the proffered hand. "Hello Lily, what can I do for you?"

The young brows knitted together in concern. "I know you're Alan's aunt. I wanted to ask your advice. I've been really worried about what I should do ever since it happened."

Indigo glanced around. They were alone in the space between the club house and the car park. "By 'it' you mean the murder?"

The other nodded, took a deep breath, released it, took another, and spoke disjointedly. "You see Alan was with me that morning, only he wasn't with me when it happened. Or, at least, I don't think he was. So I don't know whether it's best for Alan if I say he was with me or not." She looked at Indigo hopefully.

"Okay. What time was he with you?"

"We met up around eight thirty, but I don't know how long we were together. Not long, I don't think. We were just making arrangements for that evening." She blinked, her eyes filling with tears. "Maybe I should just say he was with me the whole time."

"Lying isn't going to help," she said gently. "I take it Alan's your boyfriend?"

Lily nodded and brushed at her eyes with the back of her hand. "We met when he came to join the protestors. I was walking my dog in the woods and he stopped to pet her."

She studied the girl, trying to judge her motive for approaching her like this. "I don't understand why Alan hasn't said he was with you. If he was."

"He was," insisted Lily. "The idiot's trying to protect me. You see, I told him I didn't want my father to know I was seeing him. You don't know what it's like. Dad snaps at any male who comes within five feet of me or my sister Rose. I don't like sneaking around, but I wouldn't have a life otherwise."

Indigo paused, considering the original question. Would it be better or worse to explain what Alan had been doing in the woods that morning? "I think you should tell the police," she said at last. "I can give you the phone number for Inspector Howard. He'll give you a sympathetic hearing."

"Will it help, though, even if I don't know when he left me?"

"Yes, definitely. You see, a trained investigator can tell Alan's hiding something. At the moment that's just making him look guilty."

"But, won't they just say he bumped into that man on the way back to camp and had a row with him?"

"It didn't happen like that. We've proved Taylor was killed at the other end of the woods. Believe me, Lily, if the case gets to court your testimony will help Alan's defence."

The girl sprang forward and flung her arms around her. "Oh, thank you. I knew you'd know what to do. Alan said you could be trusted."

Indigo took hold of her shoulders and held her at arms length so she could see her face. "You've spoken to Alan?"

"They let him phone me."

"Recently?"

"Yesterday. He told me about the beating, it's really shaken him up. He'd written, saying I shouldn't get involved, but I told him I can't keep quiet if he's getting hurt. That's why he said I should talk to you."

She took out one of her own business cards and wrote Howard's name and number on the back. "Talk to the inspector," she said. "Just tell him the truth. If you need me, ring the number on the front. If I'm not there, my PA will take a message."

Lily took the card and walked in the direction of the hotel, almost skipping as she went. Indigo followed her with her eyes, her heart sinking as she remembered the interview she'd just left. Oh hell. What if the only way to release Lily's boyfriend was to have her father arrested?

Chapter Thirteen

Her next appointment was the following morning, with Derian Winslow at the Oxely District Civic Centre in Great Oxing. This time there was no opportunity to pump a subordinate as Winslow came down to fetch her himself. She wondered for a moment if this was a deliberate ploy, but quickly realised it was the great man demonstrating his common touch.

"Well, well," he said as they travelled up in the lift, "it's not often I get to meet a real private investigator."

Not often, she thought, what a strange thing to say. She gave a bland smile and told him how pleased she was he'd agreed to see her.

"Just doing my duty. As a member of the council's senior management team I feel I ought to uphold the rights of the defence."

"Quite," she murmured.

Winslow's office was larger than she'd expected, but neat and tidy, with good quality furniture. There were neither photos nor certificates on the walls, but some rather nice pieces of artwork. He saw her looking at them and gave a smile of approval as he led her to an area of soft seating and gestured for her to sit. "Our Sport and Culture Division has a small collection of paintings available on loan to senior managers."

"How useful," she replied politely, sinking into a disturbingly deep easy chair. She was beginning to sound idiotic, but there was something about the man that overwhelmed her. That air of easy superiority was making her feel self-conscious.

Trying to ignore the effect he was having, she focused on her reason for being there and studied him dispassionately. His clothes were every bit as expensive as she'd thought at H&G and she wondered if he was one of those local government managers who earned more than the Prime Minister. He certainly gave the impression of being very high up in the hierarchy, but she didn't know enough about the workings of local government to know if that was so.

"Would you like something to drink?" he asked. "I can get my PA to make you a tea or coffee."

"Thank you, no." She paused while he lowered himself into the seat next to hers, then launched into her questioning. "Mr Winslow, I'm following up the numbers in Peter Taylor's telephone log. Trying to piece together what he was doing in the last days of his life. I see you spoke to him several times during that last week."

"Oh yes, of course." He leant back and casually crossed his right leg over his left, resting his hands comfortably on his thighs. "He wanted to put a paper before the Planning Committee. Technically, only officers can present papers to a council committee, but I look upon Henckle and Green as partners in the bypass project, so I offered to sponsor it for him. In essence, putting it forward as if it came from my Division."

She was annoyed that his position meant she had to twist uncomfortably if she wanted to see his face. "This paper," she said, "it was arguing for a change back to the original route?"

He gave a little nod. "To be honest, it wouldn't have been passed. Our original submission on the route change was quite comprehensive. Taylor didn't have anything to add except that H&G couldn't afford the alteration." He gave a little laugh. "Which isn't the council's problem, of course. They should have allowed for changes when they made their bid for the contract."

"But surely it's going to take longer if they have to dig up the woodland?"

He shifted slightly in his seat. "Who told you that?"

"Eleanor Knight."

"Eleanor's a Marketing Manager, she doesn't understand planning matters. Take it from me, there were very good reasons for making that slight alteration to the original route."

For one awful moment, Indigo thought he was going to pat her on the knee. She found it dreadfully unnerving to be around such total self-belief. "If you look on H&G as partners, why won't you allow them to increase the price to cover the extra costs?"

"We couldn't do that, it would invalidate the tender process." He uncrossed his legs and sat upright. "Look, public service organisations have to be very careful in awarding contracts, especially construction contracts. The point is to ensure complete fairness and transparency. How fair would it be if we awarded a contract on the basis of H&G's price and then allowed them to ask for more money?"

"But the route they bid on has changed."

"It's only a small change, and it's covered by clause 26, paragraph 4 of the contract."

No wonder Eleanor Knight had been so infuriated after her meeting with him. He could probably quote a clause and paragraph for any objection that might be raised. Was it possible they'd intended the woodland route all along and set the parameters so the change would come in under the limit of that wretched clause? Or was she becoming paranoid?

She changed the subject. "I hope you don't mind me asking, but are you a member of Great Oxing Country Club?"

"Oh yes, naturally, it's a top class club."

"So you play golf?"

He lowered his eyes in a display of feigned humility. "I'm a fair player. Of course, I don't have time to play a lot, but I do get in the occasional round with some of the Councillors."

"Including Councillor Porter?"

"As it happens, yes. Bill Porter likes a game of golf now and then." He leant towards her with a smile that suggested he was favouring her with a closely-guarded secret. "He's not very good, you know, so I have to play below my best."

So, he let Porter win, did he? That told her an awful lot more about Winslow than he meant to reveal. But the interview was getting her absolutely nowhere. "Well, thank you," she said. "I won't take up any more of your time. A man in your position must have a lot to do."

She'd said the right thing. He beamed at her and jumped to his feet, holding out a hand to help her out of the chair. For one moment she thought of refusing his help, but the soft stuffing clung to her like a suction pad. It was either accept his help or struggle inelegantly to her feet like an old woman. She took his hand and allowed him to help her up, not even flinching when he put his hand on her shoulder as he guided her towards the door.

"You won't mind if I don't come down with you," he said as they shook hands. "As you say, I have a lot of work to catch up with."

"Don't worry, I can find my own way."

He took hold of the door handle, then stopped and gave her a sad little smile. "I was sorry to hear about Taylor," he said. "He had a good reputation in town planning circles. Ironically, I drove past those woods the morning he was murdered." He gave an artistic little shudder. "Isn't that strange? I don't usually take that route because getting through Aldgate is such hell, but I had to drop my partner off at her office that morning."

"Did you see anything unusual?" she asked. "A parked car, maybe?"

He opened the door and stood back. "Nothing, I'm afraid. I would have contacted the police if I'd had any information to offer. Naturally."

"Naturally," she echoed and hurried out, pleased to be free.

On the way down in the lift she told herself it should be possible to arrest people for arrogance and stupidity. And what was all that about driving past the woods on the day of the murder? Chances were he was on the other side of town but wanted to inject himself into the little local drama. The man was a patronising poseur, who hadn't told her anything she didn't already know. Except that he'd confirmed her suspicion that both he and Councillor Porter were members of the Country Club. As, it would appear, were several other Oxely District Councillors. She wasn't sure what it meant, only that Spencer-Cooper was worried about it.

By the end of that day, Maisie had still not been able to secure an appointment with Councillor Porter and gave it as her considered opinion that he was trying to avoid her. Indigo decided to try and corner him at his place of work. She knew he was owner and CEO of a small plastics factory based on an industrial estate eight miles to the North of Great Oxing, and thought the best time to attack was early the next morning.

As she drove to the site her only concern was about the level of security employed. If it was too good she wouldn't get near Porter and would have to consider hanging around his house, which she was loath to do. But the initial entry to the factory proved remarkably easy. She'd deliberately arrived at clocking on time and simply slipped into the line of cars passing through the factory gates. The security guard sat in his little box looking bored, and she gave him a cheeky wave as she passed.

The next obstacle was getting into the building without going through the reception area, where she would undoubtedly be asked if she had an appointment. Once again she joined a line of workers. The two staff entrances had key codes, but it was easy enough to put her hand out and stop the door closing behind the person in front of her.

So far, so good, but now came the tricky task of finding Bill Porter. She headed past the double doors leading into one of the factory areas and made for the offices at the rear of the building. The office doors were labelled and she soon found the one marked W. A. Porter CEO, though not without getting a few suspicious looks from arriving office staff. She smiled at them, straightened her shoulders, grasped the door handle, and walked in.

Except this wasn't Bill Porter's office, it was the office of his secretary. The woman looked up from her keyboard, frowned and said, "Who are you and what are you doing in this office?"

She tried a bluff. "I have an appointment to see Mr Porter."

The secretary was in her early sixties, and had probably started work at Porter's Plastics when the councillor's father was running the place. The thin, barely-wrinkled face and iron-grey hair gave her an unyielding look. She raised a well-kept eyebrow at Indigo. "No, you haven't. I'm fully aware of Mr Porter's schedule for the day." She reached towards the telephone. "I don't know how you got in, but I'm going to have you removed."

Indigo placed her hand on the receiver, holding it down, and lowered her head to look directly into the grey eyes. "I'm here to talk to the councillor about a murder. Either he talks to me now or he has a whole bunch of journalists outside asking what he said to Peter K. Taylor two days before his death."

It came down to a staring match, and the secretary was good. Indigo, however, had learnt to outstare even the toughest drug dealer and she ignored the strained position of her neck for a good ten minutes until the other woman sighed and lowered her eyes.

"Tell me your name and I'll see if he can spare you five minutes." It was a grudging acceptance of defeat.

"Give him this." She took out one of her cards and wrote on the back 'Why are you too scared to tell me what Peter Taylor said to you?'.

The woman took the card, read the message, glared at her, but made no further attempt to pick up the phone. Indigo stepped back to allow her to slip out from behind her desk and disappear through the door to Porter's office. Thank goodness she'd had the sense to back down. She could have made a nasty scene, but that wouldn't have looked good, of course. Or was she going to phone security from Porter's office? It was a possibility.

A few minutes later, however, she reappeared and held the door open. "He'll see you."

Indigo thanked her politely and stepped through the door, hearing it click quietly closed behind her. The room was very much a working office, more so than those of the other executives she'd visited on this case. Bill Porter was standing behind his desk, back to the window, his expression angry. He was around the same age as Spencer-Cooper, maybe a year or two younger. Their heights were about the same, but Porter was heavier, bordering on fatness. Too many corporate lunches, she thought, noting the ruddy complexion that clashed with his sandy hair.

"What the hell do you mean by this?" he shouted at her, waving the business card in his hand.

She could see this interview was going to be conducted standing up and planted her feet squarely on the thick carpet, as if grounding herself ready to face an onslaught. "Just what it says, Mr Porter. My secretary has been trying to get a meeting for me since the day before yesterday and you've been stonewalling. I just want to ask a few simple questions, which you obviously don't want to answer. Why is that?"

"I don't know anything." He stepped away from the window, bringing him to the side of his desk and closer to her. Menacingly so. "This is just a waste of my time."

"All I want know is why Taylor called you," she said evenly. "You know that much."

"Taylor! Damn the man!" The name seemed to enrage him even more. "You want to know why he called me? I'll tell you why he called me. He wanted an appointment so he could insult me. Insult me in public, in front of all the Council Members. That's why he called me."

Uh oh, did she sense another Taylor argument? For an inoffensive man he really knew how to rub people up the wrong way. It was a wonder he hadn't got himself killed before this, if he had such an affect on those he met.

"In what way did he insult you?"

He glared at her and threw her card into a nearby waste bin, the action seeming to dissipate his fury slightly. "If you must know," he growled as deeper spots of red appeared on his cheeks, "he accused me of taking a bribe."

Things suddenly began to make a lot more sense. "Let me see if I understand," she said. "Peter Taylor arranged to meet you in the Council Chamber, and accused you of taking a bribe from Ronald Spencer-Cooper to change the route of the bypass away from his club. Is that what happened?"

"That's about the size of it," he admitted reluctantly. "Me, accepting a bribe. I've never been so insulted in my life."

She grimaced in sympathy. "It wasn't very tactful of him to do it in public like that."

"It was downright impertinent of him to do it at all."

"Did he offer any proof?"

The hackles, which had been smoothing down, rose in fury again. "Proof! How could he prove something that wasn't true? It was slander, pure slander. I consulted my solicitor, but he talked me out of suing. Said it would only make things worse." He took another step towards her and jabbed a finger in her direction. "You dare say anything about this to the press and I will sue. You and them. You mark my words."

She eyed the blood suffused face warily. This probably wasn't the best time to ask for an alibi. Not that he'd actually attack her, and he was no match for her martial arts skills in any case. But there was no point in provoking him into a heart attack by pushing him further.

"Okay," she said quietly, "that's really all I needed to know." She gave him what she hoped was a calming smile. "You've helped me a lot. Now I know the way Taylor's mind was working, I can put some of the pieces into place."

"The way his mind was working? He, he —" Porter was lost for a way to describe what he thought of Taylor's mind and she used his confusion to back to the door and slide outside.

"I hope you haven't upset him too much," said the secretary, who was hovering so close that Indigo almost bumped into her.

"It's not my fault your boss overreacts," she replied, meeting the grey eyes steadily. "Perhaps you'd better go in and calm him down."

She could see the woman was torn, but she shook her head and stepped past Indigo towards the corridor. "Oh no, I'm escorting you out of the building, and I suggest you don't come back again."

Chapter Fourteen

Despite the difficult interview with Bill Porter, Indigo was feeling more optimistic as she drove back to the agency. Things really did seem to be coming into focus. If Taylor had accused Porter of accepting a bribe to allow the route change, it was odds on he'd also accused Ronald Spencer-Cooper of giving that bribe. Naturally Porter would say there was no proof of such a deal, but what if Taylor had found proof? Bribing a public official was a criminal offence. If Spencer-Cooper had had a good motive for killing Taylor before, he had an even better one now.

She was humming to herself again as she entered the outer office. Maisie looked up from her keyboard and smiled at her.

"That went well, then?"

She sauntered across to Maisie's desk, pulled up a chair and dropped into it, crossing her legs in a comfortable position. "Difficult to get in, but worth the effort. Taylor apparently accused Porter of taking a bribe from Spencer-Cooper."

"Really? Well, that is interesting."

There was an odd tone in Maisie's voice that caused Indigo to study her more closely. "Okay, what's happened?"

Her friend arched her eyebrows in a teasing expression. "I had a very strange telephone call while you were out."

"Strange? In what way? From whom?"

"No idea, pet. When I asked for her name she went all unnecessary. You can hear for yourself."

Indigo gave a nod to signify both understanding and agreement. The agency recorded all telephone calls, not only to protect against false accusations or legal claims, but also to enable a review of what had actually been said. It was the same logic behind the way in which she and her investigators tried to record all their interviews. Now, Maisie reached out and played back the recording, using the speaker facility to enable Indigo to listen in.

Indigo uncrossed her legs and leant forward, listening closely as the voices of Maisie and an unknown woman filled the air.

"Lattimer Investigations. How can I help you?"

"Is that Indigo Lattimer?"

"Miss Lattimer is out at the moment. I'm her Personal Assistant. Maybe I can help?"

"I ... yes, I suppose so. Can you give Miss Lattimer a message?"

"Certainly. Or I could take your details —"

"No, no ... please, just take a message."

"Okay, if that's what you'd prefer."

"Tell her someone was driving past Oxley Woods on the morning of the murder and saw Ronald Spencer-Cooper come out of the woods looking furtive."

"Furtive?"

"He threw something into the weeds, something small and metal."

"That could —"

"It was near the signpost. About two feet from the signpost."

"But —"

Then the click as the phone was replaced.

"Well," asked Maisie as the recording ended, "what do you make of that?"

"I think it's the first time I've ever heard you speechless."

Maisie threw a pencil sharpener at her head which she dodged easily, holding her hands up in surrender. "Okay, I'll be serious. Yes, you're right, it's very interesting. But, as you tried to say, there could be many innocent explanations for Spencer-Cooper being in the woods."

"The wretched woman put the phone down before I could get a better fix on where the bloke was supposed to have dropped this evidence. It could be any signpost."

"No it couldn't, there are only two on that side of the road. One's at the lay-by and gives parking regulations. If anything had been dropped near there, the SOCO team would have found it after I alerted them to the phone. The other one's just beyond the area where the body was found. It says 'Lay-by 500 metres'. That's probably the one she meant."

"You're going to follow up then?"

"Oh, I think so, given the way my suspicions are tending." Despite Maisie's sudden look of interest, she didn't elaborate. Instead she sat chewing a fingernail for a few minutes, then reached for the phone on Maisie's desk. George answered almost immediately.

"It's Indie," she said. "If you have a few minutes, I'd like you to listen to the recording of a phone call Maisie took earlier today." Having got his agreement, she played the recording down the phone to him. "Well," she asked after it ended, "what do you think?"

There was a silence at the other end. She could imagine him weighing up the alternatives carefully before deciding on the best answer. "It could be a crank call," he said at last. "We get them all the time."

"I'm not immune to them myself," she replied. "You'd be amazed the effect the words 'private investigator' have on some people. Still, I'm impressed by the way she said 'the murder' without elaboration. She was very focussed about what she wanted to say."

"Even if Spencer-Cooper was seen coming out of the woods, it doesn't mean anything. His club's just opposite. For all we know he could take a regular morning walk in the woods."

"Give me a break." She glared at the handset. "The man has two full sized golf courses to walk round if he feels the need for exercise. Never mind. I just thought I ought to let you know about the call and give you the chance to join me. Don't worry, I can take Rupert out there again."

To her surprise she heard laughter, then he said, "Whoa, slow down Indie. I didn't say I wouldn't come and take a look. If I don't, you'll be phoning me in an hour to say you've found the murder weapon. I'll meet you by the signpost."

"You know —"

"I know there are two, but the one nearest the body dump seems most likely. Don't you think?"

She agreed and said goodbye.

She found him already waiting when she arrived and was unaccountably annoyed. His office was further away from the woods than the agency so she should have got there first. For a moment she suspected him of using his siren to get ahead of her, then gave herself a mental shake and told herself to get a grip. She'd called him on his mobile rather than his office phone, so he could have been anywhere in West Sussex. Why was this whole situation with him making her a little crazy?

He was leaning against the bonnet of his car, looking relaxed. It made her realise how tense he'd seemed at their last two meetings. Was that because of the break-up, or could it be to do with DCI Waters' approach to this case? George was most definitely what they called a straight arrow and he wouldn't like any rush to judgement. It was a good job he hadn't known of Alan's relationship to herself in the beginning.

She parked her car behind his and walked forward to join him. He was already wearing gloves and shoe covers, and he watched silently as she donned her own. Then he nodded a greeting and stood up. "You still haven't come in to make that statement about the lay-by," he reminded her.

No, she hadn't. She hadn't known how to approach him now he was an ex-lover. Just being this close to him was causing an ache around her ribs. "How do you want to go about this?" she asked, ducking the issue again.

"How about we start two foot behind that sign and each take one side to search?"

That made her chuckle. "That's very equitable of you."

A smile lit his eyes. "Always happy to help the defence."

For a moment she had an image of him standing at her door on their first date, that same smile on his face. It made her gasp and she put a hand on his arm to stop him walking away. "George, I'm sorry."

The smile was replaced by a frown. "Sorry for what?"

That brought her up short. What was she sorry for? Sorry for being Alan's aunt? Sorry George cared so little for her that he'd been able to break up without a moment's thought? Sorry that she was head-over-heels in love with him? She swallowed and her voice came out as a whisper. "I'm sorry things have turned out as they have."

Was that a flinch? If so, it was quickly replaced by his official mask. "Let's just do this search, shall we?"

She nodded, allowing him to pull free, and they set about prodding through their respective patches of ground looking for the mysterious object Spencer-Cooper was supposed to have thrown away. It was a painstaking process, carefully parting grass and weeds, ensuring every inch of ground was covered. They worked in silence, each caught up in their own thoughts, until Indigo realised she was going to have to ask the question buzzing at the back of her mind. "What happened about the lay-by? Was it the murder scene?"

He answered without looking up from his search and his tone was friendly, but not intimate. "Oh, yes, undoubtedly. That was blood you pointed out. The killer had attempted to wash it away with water, which cleaned off the gravel, but it just sank into the ground beneath. There was more than enough to account for the head wounds Taylor sustained."

"How come the police didn't check the lay-by when the body was found?"

"The honest answer?" He stopped searching and stood upright. "It never occurred to us anyone would move a body just a few hundred yards. We couldn't have scoured the whole woods anyway, they're far too big." He hesitated and his next words were said in a tone of acute embarrassment. "There was a theory Sherman had come across Taylor in town, argued with him, killed him and brought him back to the woods to conceal the body."

"Really? He just happened to be carrying the camp axe, dumped the body on his doorstep, and then drove back to town to hide the car?" The scathing comments came out before she could stop them. Damn, damn, damn. She wanted to make up with the man, not put him on the defensive. Besides which, she knew by now whose theory he was expounding.

He didn't respond to the provocation, merely bent and continued his search, but she could see from the set of his shoulders that she'd hit home. "Killers don't always act sensibly."

She made no reply and they worked in a strained silence for a while until she thought of another question. "Did you find anything other than the blood and phone in the lay-by?"

"You mean anything to clear Alan?" He shook his head and moved forward a few inches. "We found a scrap of plastic. Probably a corner from the sheet used to wrap the body. At least we know what type of plastic it was now. We also found cigarette ends, sweet wrappers, the usual things. Oh, and three used condoms. It looks like that little indent gets a lot of traffic."

He hadn't meant it humorously, but it made her laugh and he realised what he'd said, throwing her a wry glance that eased the tension. She moved on to the next patch of weeds and pulled the branches of a small bush aside, causing something to rattle and fall to the ground. Carefully completing the action, she looked down to find a set of keys lying on the earth beneath the plant.

"George, I think I've found something."

He left his own search and came over. Crouching down beside her he peered at the spot beneath the bush. "Keys, now that's interesting." He leant forwards to get a closer look at the leather fob attached to the key ring and she pulled the branch further back so as not to scratch him. "Honda car keys." He turned his head to look up at her. "You understand the implication?"

"Taylor drove a Honda Accord."

"It could just be a massive coincidence," he warned, then gave a deep sigh. "I'll have to get the SOCO boys out here again, which will not make me popular." He stood up and waved at her to release the bush. "Once the team have retrieved them, the keys will have to be checked against Taylor's car."

She placed the branch carefully back into position so as not to disturb anything and straightened up beside him. A twinge in her back told her she was getting out of condition. She'd been so busy these past few months, she hadn't even kept up with Judo practice. She rubbed at the spot absently. "And if they are Taylor's keys, what will you do? Will you interrogate Ronald Spencer-Cooper?"

"We'd probably want to talk to Spencer-Cooper, yes, but we only have that anonymous phone call linking him to these keys." He glanced sideways at her. "I know how hard you're trying, but we don't have anything yet to point us away from Alan. Unless we can demonstrate a case against someone else, DCI Waters isn't going to give up his best suspect."

She tried not to glower, but the single-mindedness of his superior was beginning to get to her. "This is ridiculous. I've already found enough for a good barrister to get a verdict of innocent in court."

"The benefit of the doubt, there's plenty of that." He ran his fingers through his hair, the latex gloves leaving it sticking up in little peaks. "That's not what you and your sister need, is it? You need him released as soon as possible."

"You can't blame us. Alan's a complete innocent, and too polite for his own good. He's not safe in prison."

He turned to face her and reached out to place his hands lightly on her shoulders. "I heard about the beating. I'm sorry. I hope he wasn't badly hurt."

"Bad enough." She leant forwards, meaning to give him kiss, then realised what she was doing and felt herself redden. She straightened up. "The sympathy is appreciated, but there's nothing more I can do here. I'll leave you to call your people and get the process rolling." Pulling gently away from his hands, she started picking her way through the weeds towards the road. After a few steps she stopped and glanced back over her shoulder. "You'd better flatten that hair before they arrive. You look more like you've been dragged through these bushes than searched through them."

He laughed and waved a hand as she resumed the journey to her car, wondering what her next move should be.

Chapter Fifteen

She knew she should have told him about her interviews with Spencer-Cooper and Councillor Porter. Maybe the suggestion of political corruption would have made him take Ronald Spencer-Cooper more seriously as a suspect. Maybe it would have swayed him, but she wasn't so sure about the shadowy figure of DCI Waters. So far he hadn't appeared in person and she was beginning to suspect George was covering for him. It was her belief the Chief Inspector had made his mind up and wasn't going to put any further personal effort into the case unless he was presented with a signed confession. She wondered fleetingly if George was going beyond his own authority on her behalf. Better to follow this lead by herself until she had something more substantial to share.

As she drove past the Country Club sign, she knew her next move. She hadn't asked Ronald Spencer-Cooper for an alibi. It was time she did so.

She turned right at the end of the road and followed the Country Club boundary until she could find a place to safely pull over and use her mobile phone. Spencer-Cooper answered on the third ring.

"Mr Spencer-Cooper, this is Indigo Lattimer. I was wondering if I could pop in and see you. I'm in the area and I just need to clear up a couple of points."

She could hear annoyance in his voice as he said, "I'm sorry Miss Lattimer. I'm very busy at the moment. Besides, I've nothing more to add to what I've already told you."

"That's a shame," she said. "I've been told you were seen in Oxley Woods around the time of the murder. Obviously, I've had to pass this information on to the police. I'm sure there's an innocent explanation and I wanted to find out what it was so I could head them off for you. Of course, I can quite understand if you'd rather speak to them about it."

There was a long silence at the other end and she allowed it to stretch until Spencer-Cooper was ready to reply. "You said you were nearby?"

"Just around the corner."

"Then I can spare you ten minutes. I assure you I wasn't in the woods that day. If you come straight round I can prove it to you."

She put down her phone and started up the car. There had been a definite hint of fear in his voice after she'd threatened him, almost a tremble. She wondered what sort of alibi he would provide.

Despite being so close. it took her almost twenty minutes to reach the entrance, find a parking space and arrive at Spencer-Cooper's office. He must have been waiting for her because he pulled the door open even before she'd finished knocking. Once again he put the desk between them as a barrier, but he didn't sit. Instead, he strode back and forth in a small square between his chair and a pair of metal cabinets. Three paces one way, three paces the other. She decided to allow him the height advantage and sat on the edge of a visitor's chair near where he was pacing.

"I wasn't in Oxley Woods on the morning of the fifth," he said without preamble. "It's ridiculous to even suppose I was. I have no reason to go into the woods." He paused long enough to glare at her. "Ever."

"That's exactly what I said to Inspector Howard," she said innocently. "Mr Spencer-Cooper has two golf courses to walk round if he needs exercise. Why would he want to walk in the woods?"

"And a fitness suite in the hotel," he muttered.

"Precisely," she agreed. "So, where were you that morning?"

"I was on the A course, playing a round of golf with my course manager, Barry Raven. The A course is on the opposite side of the club to the woods. This witness of yours, whoever they might be, is totally mistaken. I was nowhere near the woods."

"I take it Mr Raven will confirm this round of golf?"

He stopped pacing and turned to face her, squaring his shoulders and donning an expression of resigned good humour. "There's no reason why I should let you pester Barry, but just to get you off my back I've asked him if he'll speak with you. His office is just next door. Now, if you'll excuse me, I'm busy."

He made as if to lead her to the door, but she didn't move.

"Not so fast," she said. "I want to know why you lied to me at our last meeting."

"Lied?" His right hand clenched into a fist, and she could see his finger nails digging into the skin of his palm.

"You told me Taylor spoke to you about the Compulsory Purchase Order, but that's not true, is it? He really came to accuse you of bribing Councillor Porter."

Spencer-Cooper drew in a sharp breath and held it so long she thought he'd pass out if he didn't take another soon. His eyes darted around the room. Now, was he going to make a break for it or was he planning an attack? Those golf clubs looked like they'd make handy weapons if he was desperate enough.

He did neither. Letting the air out in a long, noisy gasp, he said, "That's not true. I don't know where you got that idea from. I told you what he wanted with me. I got angry with him because he disparaged my golf courses. He was a very rude man. Now, please, talk to Barry and get out of my life."

She decided to let it go. His initial reaction had been enough to confirm her suspicions to her own satisfaction. Once she handed her evidence over to the police they'd be able to get access to his bank account, and that of Bill Porter. That would show if any money had changed hands. Or maybe it was something other than money? No matter, if there had been bribery the police would root it out.

She stood up and walked to the door. He made no further attempt to accompany her, remaining behind his desk, watching her warily. She opened the door and stepped outside. As she closed it, she glanced back into the room. He'd slumped into his chair with his forehead resting on his desk in an attitude of defeat.

She had no problem finding the office of Barry Raven. It was, as Spencer-Cooper had said, the next door along the corridor. She knocked as loudly as she could, wondering what kind of a reception she'd get. A voice called "Come in" and she entered.

Barry Raven was younger, thinner and fitter than his employer. He had the look of a man who spent the majority of his time outdoors and she thought the role of course manager might be quite a pleasant one if you liked golf. He smiled up at her from the pile of papers on his desk and asked, "Miss Lattimer? Ronnie asked me if I'd have a word with you. How can I help?'

He seemed genuinely friendly, but there was something in his eyes. Not wariness, exactly. Discomfort maybe. She was sure any alibi he provided must be false and it couldn't be easy being asked to lie for the boss. She made an instant decision not to confront him about what he told her. The police could do that once she'd pushed them in the right direction. Enough now to hear what had been concocted.

"Mr Spencer-Cooper tells me you and he played a round of golf on the morning of the fifth of August. Can you confirm that?"

He sat back in his chair, the picture of comfort. "Oh, certainly. Ronnie and I often take advantage of a gap in reservations to get in a quick round."

"And you're sure you played that morning?"

"Absolutely certain."

You would be, she thought, if you've been roped in as an alibi. "That was the B course, wasn't it?"

"The A course. It's difficult to get a gap on the B course because it's so popular."

Damn, they might have had only minutes to come up with a story, but he had it off pat. She found her confidence in the falsity of this alibi wavering. What if Raven was telling the truth and Spencer-Cooper wasn't in the woods that morning? She took a breath. "Was Mr Spencer-Cooper out of your sight at any point during that game?"

He looked momentarily flustered and came back upright. "Out of my sight? I don't understand."

So, you weren't anticipating that question, she thought. She clarified her meaning. "Did he go off into the rough to retrieve a ball, or maybe he was called back to the clubhouse for a while."

"No." He became more confident. "No, Ronnie's too good a player to need to look for a ball. And people know not to disturb us when we're on the green."

"I see."

He hadn't offered her a seat, or shaken her hand, so now she just nodded, thanked him for his time and left the office.

She walked out into the bar area feeling frustrated. She still didn't have anything but suspicions and she wasn't sure whether those would be enough to push the police into action. She looked up and realised the same bar steward was on duty as on her previous visit. What's more, her stomach was grumbling. She glanced at the clock. It was nearly lunchtime and she'd missed breakfast that morning in order to get to Porter's for clocking on time.

She walked over to the bar. "Hi, remember me?"

He nodded, but didn't look pleased to see her . "A good barman never forgets a face. You're the woman who was asking about that dead man."

"That's right. I've just been talking with the governor again. Look, I always seem to be missing meals at the moment, and I'm starving. Is there any chance of getting another one of those delicious sandwiches?"

"We don't open until noon."

She put on her best wheedling voice. "Maybe I could get one to take with me?"

He thought about it, relented with a shrug and went to pass her order through the archway. As he was dealing with her money she said, "Mr Spencer-Cooper was telling me about a game of golf he had with Mr Raven. I expect they play together a lot, having the facilities at hand like they do."

"They play. I wouldn't say a lot. They're both busy men."

"Of course." She put her change away carefully. "I suppose Mr Raven usually wins? He's the course manager, after all."

He scowled at her, showing he hadn't forgiven her for trying to get him to break a confidence the last time. "Then you'd be wrong. The boss man has a scratch handicap on the A course and an 8 on the B course. He wins about three games to every one of Mr Raven's."

There was a call from the food preparation area and Indigo waited until he returned with her sandwich before saying, "Who won on the fifth of August?"

He handed her the package and stood silently for a moment. "Neither," he said at last, with a smirk at having caught her out in a mistake. "They couldn't have played on the fifth. Mr Raven was on holiday the first two weeks of August. He went to France."

She had great difficulty in stopping herself from showing jubilation at his reply. Yes! Raven had been lying to protect his boss, and the police would be able to prove it. Spencer-Cooper had played right into her hands.

Forcing herself to look crestfallen she said, "Sorry, I must have misheard. I have no memory for dates. Thank you for the sandwich. You're a life saver" She threw him a beaming smile in the hope of keeping him on side for any future occasion and walked casually out of the clubhouse.

Chapter Sixteen

By the time she reached the office, she was feeling jubilant. Catching Spencer-Cooper in that lie was the piece of the jigsaw she felt sure would get the police thinking again about the murder. She was whistling a tune to herself as she entered, which caught Maisie's attention.

"Having a good day, are we?"

"Yes, I think we are. I'm just going to fill some things in on the chart. Where's Rupert by the way?"

"Out doing the next batch of Mystery Shopper stores. I can come and act as cardboard cut-out if you want."

Indigo laughed and shook her head. The cardboard cut-out was an agency joke. It referred to the way problems suddenly became clear when you tried to explain them to someone else, even if they only stood and nodded.

"I don't need a cardboard cut-out," she told Maisie, "but you can bring a couple of cups of coffee into the conference room and listen to what I've got."

"Have you eaten?"

"I brought a sandwich back from the Country Club. I'll have it with my coffee."

While Maisie was making the coffee, Indigo added information to the whiteboard. Rupert had already created columns for the three new names they'd gotten from Taylor's phone log. Now she filled in the blanks. To her surprise, all three men fitted the general description – thirties, brown hair, clean shaven, around five foot ten. Though, come to think of it, Spencer-Cooper was probably in his forties given the age of his daughter. Still, close enough given the fleeting glance Mrs Hunter had had. It would seem her description was a lot vaguer than it had first appeared. She filled in the space marked 'alibi' by putting 'false' for Spencer-Cooper, 'driving partner' for

Winslow, and a question mark for Porter. Rupert had added another row – 'motive'. Against this Indigo put 'bribery' for both Spencer-Cooper and Porter, but a dash for Winslow because there didn't seem any reason for him to harm Taylor.

"Lots of information," said Maisie coming in with the coffee. "What does it tell you?"

Indigo took the cup being offered, sat down at the table, and unwrapped her sandwich. "It tells me Ronald Spencer-Cooper is our number one suspect." She took a bite of her sandwich, decided against talking with her mouth full, and sat contentedly eating and drinking while Maisie studied the board.

Only when Indigo had finished her meal did Maisie say, "Well, the bloke has a lot going against him alright. How'd you get all that?"

Indigo gave her a summary of her interviews over the past two days and finished by saying, "Add that to the telephone call, and George and I finding what could be Taylor's car keys, and I think there's a pretty good case for Mr Spencer-Cooper to answer. Don't you?'

"And what does George think?" the other asked, putting unnecessary emphasis on the forename.

Maisie was talking as if they were still a couple, probably hoping things could be straightened out. But this wasn't the time to be discussing the situation. Not with the case still going on and the feeling George was still working against her. Nothing she'd given him so far exonerated Alan, but only helped him build his case. She had to pin down an alternative case against Spencer-Cooper.

She stood abruptly and pushed her chair under the meeting room table. "I need my latest interviews downloaded," she said firmly.

Her PA followed her meekly out to her own desk in the reception area and took the phone held out to her. Plugging it into her computer, she started downloading the day's sound recordings in silence.

"If you could transcribe all the interviews onto a USB stick by mid-morning tomorrow, I'll take my evidence along to Inspector Howard and see if I can spring Alan from that wretched jail." She put her own emphasis on the name as a warning to back off on the relationship front.

The other ignored the provocation and watched the download with an air of resignation until the little blue bar was complete. Then she detached the phone and handed it back. "I suppose most of them were recorded from your pocket and will be all weak and indistinct?"

Indigo took it with a chuckle and slipped it back into the offending pocket. "Not at all. I hold it in my hand whenever I can. Besides, you know you're a genius at deciphering my recordings and boosting the volume."

Maisie grunted and settled herself behind her desk. "I have to be. You have far too many conversations with people who don't want to be recorded." She met Indigo's eyes. "I'll start on these right away, but I can't guarantee you'll get them before midday. What are you going to do?"

"I'm going to have an early night. Catching a murderer is a lot harder on the nerves than tracking a missing teenager. I think I deserve to leave an hour early."

"Uh, it's alright for some. I'll be here till seven again, transcribing those interviews."

She shook her head, but didn't answer. Maisie wouldn't be staying late because it was the night her mother-in-law babysat while she and Rod had their weekly date night. Only a major emergency would make her miss that to work late. Indigo retrieved various belongings from her office, then headed out of the door and made her way down the stairs for the walk to the back of the building and her car. She was feeling pleased with herself. There had been a point when she thought herself not up to the case, but logical methods and a little bit of luck had won out in the end.

Midnight was flat out in the shade at the side of the cabin, sleeping contentedly. Indigo made no attempt to disturb her, but put fresh water in her bowl. Then she stopped, stood for a moment studying the sleeping cat, and went to get a sachet of food. It hadn't been asked for, but she was feeling expansive and generous this evening.

Then she turned to her own needs, the first of which was a shower. The water felt good against her skin, warming and easing aching muscles. She hadn't realised how tense she'd been over her nephew's plight until this moment, when it looked like she might finally be able to get him released.

After she'd changed into clean jeans and a bright red-and-yellow top, she made for the kitchen. So much of her working life was spent eating on the run that she liked to cook when she had the chance. Nothing fancy, mainly what she thought of as peasant food, hot and filling. Tonight she made a big cottage pie with lots of thick gravy and served with peas, carrots and broccoli. She took her time over eating it, then went out and spent a couple of hours in her garden, dealing with the weeds she'd missed the previous Sunday.

When the light faded she retired to the lounge and picked up the novel she'd been reading before she set off to find Chloe Fielding. It was a struggle to get back into it and she wondered whether to start again from the beginning. Deciding she couldn't be bothered, she tossed it aside and turned on the radio instead. She'd never owned a television, but the radio provided just enough contact with the world at large to suit her needs. She settled back, closed her eyes, and let the sounds wash over her, only half listening. She didn't even react when a small body landed on the sofa, turned round three times, and curled up against her leg.

She was just beginning to think it was time for bed when her doorbell rang. She glanced at the clock, surprised. She hardly ever had visitors, apart from an occasional family member, and not even they called at eleven thirty at night. She wondered if it could be Rupert. He'd been known to lock himself out of the studio after a night out and she kept a spare key just in case. She stepped out into the hall and switched on the light to illuminate the blackness beyond the length of glass. Glaring in at her was a figure who'd once been a frequent visitor to her home.

"George!" she exclaimed and hurried forwards to slide the glass door open.

His brow was furrowed and waves of anger preceded him as he stepped past her and walked through the archway into her living room. Puzzled and beginning to worry slightly, she slid the door to and followed him. She found him standing in the middle of the floor, staring at her small dining table as if it would answer whatever was troubling him.

Before she could ask him any questions, he spun towards her and demanded, "What did you say to Ronald Spencer-Cooper today?"

The tone was ferocious, making her heart beat faster. Now what? Was he angry because she'd interviewed the country club owner before the police could? Even to her own ears her voice sounded unnaturally timid when she answered. "I just asked him where he was at the time of the murder. Why? Has he made an official complaint about me?"

"He's in no state to complain about anyone, he's in a coma in Great Oxing Hospital. The doctors don't know if he'll survive."

She put a hand to her mouth. "Oh my God, don't tell me he tried to commit suicide?"

He appeared to see her for the first time and registered her expression. He gave a loud sigh and all the anger drained from his body to be replaced by contrition. He raised his right hand and took a step towards her. "Indie, I'm sorry. I didn't mean to shout at you." The hand hovered over her shoulder, then he changed his mind and let it drop to his side. "He was attacked in his office this evening. He was found a little after eight by Barry Raven."

"The course manager?"

He inclined his head in the merest hint of a nod. "Spencer-Cooper was beaten about the head with a golf club. One of the more hefty ones, don't ask me what they're called. Luckily for him, the attack was a lot less ferocious than the one that killed Taylor. Otherwise he wouldn't still be with us."

"The hefty ones are called irons," she said absently, remembering her thoughts in Spencer-Cooper's office that very afternoon about what useful weapons they'd make. "This doesn't make any sense. I was convinced Spencer-Cooper was the murderer."

"Apparently not," he said, looking round. "Do you mind if I sit down?"

The request startled her, reminding her of the broken state of their relationship. "Of course not." She nodded towards the two-seater sofa in the corner of her living room, thinking how weary he seemed. All that earlier tension had come back to knot the muscles of his face and shoulders. "Have you eaten? I have half a cottage pie in the fridge. I can heat it in the microwave for you."

He hesitated and gave her a look of pure guilt. "To be honest the last meal I can recall eating was breakfast, but I don't want to put you out."

She chuckled and gave him an encouraging push towards the sofa, causing Midnight to jump down and stalk out of the room, her tail stiff with indignation. "It won't take a moment. I'll make us both some tea as well."

When she returned with the plate of steaming pie and two mugs of tea he was lying back with his eyes closed. For a moment she thought he'd fallen asleep, but he opened his eyes when she placed the tray on the coffee table in front of him and took the refreshments from her gratefully.

She allowed him to eat in silence. Perched on the edge of the sofa next to him, she sipped her tea and thought over what he'd told her. How could she have been so wrong? Everything pointed to Spencer-Cooper as the killer. Her earlier elation had crashed completely. What an idiot she'd been to think she could handle a murder case, and her blind fumbling about might have got a man killed. "Pure hubris," she muttered.

"It's not your fault, you know," he said gently. "I didn't mean to imply that at all."

She looked round. He'd finished the food and was nursing the remainder of his tea. "But it is... at least," she amended, "you're right to think it might have been something I said that led to this."

"And just what did you say that could have caused our killer to target Spencer-Cooper?"

She opened her mouth, then paused. She'd been going to tell him about the bribery aspect, but couldn't see why anyone would want to attack Spencer-Cooper over that. She told him anyway, adding, "It doesn't make sense, though. If Spencer-Cooper was the one doing the bribing, I could understand him killing to keep it quiet. Councillor Porter was accused in public, so there's no point in him trying to hide anything, unless Taylor could produce proof. Do you think other members of the Planning Committee could have been bribed too?"

"It's a possibility, but from what you've said they didn't have any part in agreeing the route change, so why would he bribe them?"

"You could look into it, though, couldn't you? Check bank accounts or something?"

The furrowed brow returned momentarily. "If I wasn't working for a thick-skulled, shallow-minded, over-educated — " He shook his head irritably. "No, forget I said that. Let's just say DCI Waters is far from convinced the attack on Spencer-Cooper is related to Taylor's murder."

"What? But —" She was lost for words. How could anyone not connect the two attacks? Surely it was too much of a coincidence for two such similar attacks, on two men who'd been involved in the same enterprise, to be unrelated?

"He thinks Spencer-Cooper was attacked by a disaffected employee. Apparently a young greens keeper was sacked recently for stealing."

"Did they find his medical bracelet near the body too?" she asked waspishly.

That made him laugh, a shout of laughter that lit his eyes and eased the tension lines around his mouth. "You're right," he said, "Rick Waters does tend to accept the first suspect presented to him. But go easy on him, I was being unfair just then. He's on the fast track because of his management skills. The reality of major crime is something he struggles with. He'll either learn to deal with criminals or the guys upstairs will move him into an administrative role. It's too soon to say yet."

"In the meantime, Alan is still in jail, and still at risk."

He stood up, carrying the tray that held his empty plate and mug, and met her eyes. "I'm sorry, I tried my best." He started to walk towards the archway. "I'll put these in the kitchen, then I'll be on my way."

She waited until he emerged from the kitchen, then put her hand on his forearm. "Do you have to go? You look exhausted and it's a long drive home."

He glanced towards the bedroom door and a wistful look entered his eyes, but he shook his head. "There's still the problem of you being Alan's aunt." He took hold of her hand and gently removed it from his arm. "I don't know how things are going to work out – with the case, or between us – but I've missed you far more than I expected to."

He turned and started to leave, but she called after him. "There's something you need to know. Twenty-three years ago my sixteen-year-old brother Paul ran away from home. He got into drugs and mugged people to fund his habit. One day a victim fought back and Paul stabbed him. While he was on remand for the murder, he tied his bedsheets together and hanged himself. He was just a year younger than Alan is now."

His shoulders had tensed while she was speaking and now he half-turned and looked at her. "And you're frightened Alan will do the same?"

"He's not as tough as Paul was. And you were wrong. Despite his age, Alan is still very much a boy. Maybe this experience will toughen him up, I don't know. But Vi and I are terrified it will actually break him."

He nodded his understanding. "The attack on Spencer-Cooper has convinced me of Alan's innocence, but it'll take more than that to persuade Waters." His hand raised towards his hair, and then dropped as if he'd caught himself in a bad habit. He gave a grim smile. "I'm having to walk a thin line. But I'm still building the case for the CPS, so any hints you can give me that can be framed as part of that case I'll follow up. That's the best I can do, Indie."

She made no reply, allowing him to leave. With the door closed behind him, the place seemed suddenly empty. Even the sight of Midnight, deigning to return now the intruder had gone, failed to cheer her. It was all very well to say he'd do what he could, but the truth was she had no idea where to go from here. With a heavy heart, she tidied the lounge, washed up, and went to bed.

Chapter Seventeen

She woke at five thirty in the morning and knew her day had started. Slipping out of bed, she got ready and went to the agency without breakfast. In the early morning light the place was cold and lonely. The heating in the building was controlled by the dentist's and remained off until the first of October. Indigo paid her share of the costs in with her rent. Today, shivering in the kitchen as she made herself a cup of coffee, she thought she was overpaying.

She took her coffee into the conference room, switched on a small fan heater, and sat staring at the whiteboard while the heater hummed in the background. No matter how she looked at it, the grid pointed to Spencer-Cooper as the most likely suspect. The only explanation was that she hadn't met the real killer yet. Was she going to have to interview every person Taylor had ever come into contact with and try to guess which one he'd upset enough to kill him? No, not all, she reminded herself, just the men. She jumped up in anger and erased the grid from the board, rubbing furiously until every last trace of it was gone.

Standing in the centre of the room, looking at the blank whiteboard, she said aloud, "and that hasn't helped me one bit." She couldn't remember having felt so down for a long time. Even the knowledge that George was missing her couldn't overcome her sense of failure and frustration.

She left the conference room and went to her office. Sitting in the middle of her desk was a USB stick. The transcripts she'd asked for. Maisie must have stayed late after all and finished them before she went home. They were no use now. She picked up the stick up, meaning to put it in her drawer, then stopped. Maybe it would be worth reading them through to remind herself what had actually been said in those interviews. Perhaps something would jump out at her to suggest a new line of enquiry.

The transcripts covered both of her interviews with Spencer-Cooper, plus those with Winslow, Porter, Raven and the two conversations with the bar steward. They gave her nothing new, but they did start her wondering about her earlier interviews. Was there anything she'd heard that could be reinterpreted in the light of later knowledge? Luckily, all her interviews were transcribed by Maisie and filed in a case folder on her hard drive. Indigo went out to the reception area and switched on Maisie's computer, quickly finding the folder she wanted.

She began reading back through the interviews, starting with her conversation with Mike Nash. As she read, things occurred to her and she made notes. By the time she finished she had questions based upon the accounts of Amy Dwyer, Eleanor Knight and Mrs Barnes. Of these, she thought Amy was the person she most wanted to talk to again. If she was right, Amy could be a vital witness.

The outer door opened and Maisie entered. She was surprised to see Indigo sitting at her desk. "You're in early, pet. Anything wrong?'

Indigo looked up, feeling guilty about her friend missing her date night. "I was wrong," she said simply. "Ronald Spencer-Cooper isn't our killer. In fact, he's another victim."

"Hooley-dooley!" Maisie closed the door behind her and came to stand by the desk. "You don't mean he's dead?"

"As of last night, no. But apparently it's touch and go, so I don't know what the situation is this morning."

"What happened?"

"Someone beat him about the head with one of his golf clubs."

"Why didn't they use the axe?" asked Maisie, ever the practical sort, who would certainly keep a murder weapon in case it came in useful in the future.

Indigo stared at her. "Do you know, that's a very good question. I've always assumed the killer still had the axe and the plastic sheet. What if he didn't? What if he disposed of them somewhere and they just haven't been found yet?" She thought about Taylor's mobile phone and wondered what other clues were lying around the woods waiting to be stumbled upon.

Maisie removed her coat and crossed to hang it on the coat rack in the far corner. Coming back to stand by the desk she said, "Where does that leave you, pet? You were so sure Spencer-Cooper was the right bloke."

"Well, it's taught me a lesson," she said with a rueful smile. "These murder enquiries are a lot harder than they look, and more dangerous."

"Perhaps you should call it a day. You said yourself you've got enough to give young Alan the benefit of the doubt."

"But not enough to secure his immediate release, apparently." She jumped up and relinquished the seat to its rightful owner. "I'm not ready to concede defeat just yet. This guy's got under my skin. I'm just going back to Oxley Woods to see Amy Dwyer." She checked her pockets for phone and car keys, then opened the outer door. "Assuming she's still there, of course."

Maisie was readjusting her chair and monitor to her liking, though Indigo had barely moved them. She glanced up and said, "I always knew you were stubborn. It'll be the death of you one of these days, you mark my words. You never know when to stop pushing."

Indigo ignored her, skipped down the stairs two at a time and made for her car.

The drive to Oxley Woods was, in some ways, relatively easy. It was rush hour, but the majority of the traffic was streaming into the city while Indigo was heading out. Very little went along the lane past Oxley Woods anyway, so she had a clear path. Even the Aldgate bottleneck was blocked solid on the other side of the road, but flowing freely on her own. By the time she reached the woods she was almost cheerful.

When she got to the camp site she found a single tent remaining. It was purple with appliquéd silver stars which told her it belonged to Amy. She knew where to find her, seated on her favourite grassy bank, staring at the pond. Her layers of flimsy but colourful draperies looked too thin to keep her warm in the winter days ahead and Indigo hoped she had something warmer with her. She also noticed how thin the girl was and worried about her being out there in the woods all alone. She sat down beside her, trying to ignore the clammy feel of dew.

"Hello Indie," said Amy without turning her head.

"Hello Amy. Where are the others?"

"Abiola's gone back to college."

"And Mike?"

Amy looked round then and gave her a bright smile. "Mike has another cause. Did you know they were going to build a super-abattoir in Derbyshire?"

"No," said Indigo, "I didn't. Has Mike gone up there?"

"Yes. He left yesterday. He's going to start a new protest group. I told him he should call it 'Animals are Human Too'."

"And how did that go down?"

Amy giggled. "He told me not to follow him." Her eyes became suddenly very sad. "He said what happened to Mr Taylor and Alan was all my fault, and he didn't want me to jinx his new camp."

"That's not true." Indigo was annoyed. She could understand Nash not wanting Amy to follow him, but it was extremely cruel for a grown man to lay a guilt trip on such a vulnerable young woman. She squeezed her hand and looked into her eyes. "Listen to me. Since talking to you last I've learnt there's a lot more going on in this case than your protest group.

It's likely Mr Taylor was killed because he uncovered some political corruption, not because of the argument he had with you."

The other's eyes filled with tears. "Then why have you come back to talk to me?" she whispered.

Oh hell, why couldn't she have just come back to find out how Amy was, rather than because she wanted something? It was a pretty good bet nobody ever sought the girl out for herself. Still, it couldn't be helped, she had to find out whether her hunch was correct or not.

She pulled a clean paper hankie out of one of her pockets and handed it to the girl. "I need to go over the day of the monsters again," she said. "If I lead you, do you think you could give me the details of what you saw?"

"I was high, you know," said Amy, dabbing her eyes. "It won't make any sense."

"I think it will, if we go carefully. I'm pretty sure you weren't seeing hallucinations, just distortions of reality. Between us we might be able to get at that reality. If you're willing?"

Amy studied her for a few minutes and then gave a small nod. "What do you want me to do?"

"Just close your eyes and remember what you saw. I'll lead you through." She took out her phone and switched to record. Amy already had her eyes tightly closed and her hands gripped together, so she started. "Let's begin just after you saw the were-rabbit shall we? Can you see what you're doing?"

"I'm running," said Amy.

She sounded scared and Indigo injected a calming tone into her voice. "Okay. You stopped running after a while and sat down, didn't you?"

"Yes."

"So, you're sitting down. Where are you now?"

"Oh, I've reached the woods. I'm almost back at the camp, but I can't find the path. The bushes were scratching me and I'm out of breath, so I'm sitting on the ground, taking a rest." She opened her eyes and looked at Indigo with surprise. "I was almost home, but it was so confusing."

She nodded and patted the girl's shoulder to reassure her. "I told you it would start to make sense. Let's carry on." Amy obediently closed her eyes again and Indigo continued. "You're sitting resting after running from the were-rabbit and you see the spider monster."

"I see it."

"How big is it?"

"How big?" Amy's voice sounded doubtful.

"Is it the size of a normal spider?"

"No, it's ... it's the size of a man."

Good, thought Indigo, that's what I was hoping to hear. But she had to go carefully, she didn't want to influence Amy's answers. "How many legs does it have?"

Amy gave a little giggle. "Two, of course, and two arms." She stopped and opened her eyes again. "It's not a spider, is it?" He expression became fearful as she realised the implications.

"I don't think so, but I need to know everything you can remember about it. Please close your eyes and carry on."

"I'm frightened." She reached out and slipped her hand into Indigo's before obediently closing her eyes once more.

"Nothing's going to happen to you. This is all in the past, it can't hurt you. Now, describe the spider to me in as much detail as you can."

"It's black ... I mean," she paused as she tried to make sense of her memories, "it must be wearing black. All black. It has a hood." Her face wrinkled up but she kept her eyes closed in concentration and said doubtfully, "It has black hands."

"Gloves," Indigo reassured her. "What's it doing?"

"It's ... Oh, no, it's pulling a big cocoon and there's prey inside it."

"How do you know what's inside the cocoon?"

"I can see through it. The cocoon is almost clear, but ... but misty. I can see a man inside the cocoon." Her words came faster, as if she wanted to get through the memory as quickly as possible. Indigo let her run on. "The cocoon's very heavy. The spider's having trouble pulling it. It keeps getting caught on branches and the spider's angry. It's talking to itself. It says, 'Damn it, this is close enough'. Now it's pushed the cocoon towards a bush and the prey has fallen out. The prey is lying under the bush. I can only see the foot."

She gave a little sob. Indigo looked at her more closely and saw tears on her cheeks, but couldn't allow her to stop. She had to know everything Amy had seen. "Okay, the prey is almost hidden by the bush. What does the spider do next?"

"It folds the cocoon up." The voice became puzzled. "How strange."

"And?" prompted Indigo.

"It goes back towards the road."

"Then you lose sight of it?"

"No." She'd stopped sounding distressed and now seemed more curious. "I follow it. I'd forgotten that. I don't get too close but .... I want to see what it's going to do with the cocoon."

"And what does it do with the cocoon?"

"It has a blue lair on the road. There's a cave in the back of the lair. It takes a black rubbish sack out of the cave and puts the cocoon inside it. I think what a good spider monster it is, because it takes its rubbish away and doesn't leave it in the woods. Then it closes the cave and goes into the lair." She opened her eyes and gave Indigo a puzzled look. "The lair went away. I don't understand."

Indigo laughed. "It's alright. The blue lair was probably Taylor's car. At a guess, that cave you saw was the open boot. The killer closed the boot, got into the car and drove away. He left the car in —" A sudden realisation hit her. "Indigo Lattimer you are a complete idiot. Fool, fool, fool!"

Amy pulled her hand away from Indigo's and stared at her in astonishment.

She flashed her a quick reassuring smile. "It's alright, Amy. I've just realised something I should have realised earlier. Inspector Howard and I were told something and now I see it couldn't have been true."

"I really saw him, didn't I. The murderer?"

"I'm afraid you did. In a way, it's lucky you were high. If you'd been clear-headed you might have attracted attention to yourself." Amy shivered and she gave her a quick hug. "You've been very brave. Thank you for going through that for me."

"Did I help you?"

"Yes, you've given us information we didn't have before. Can I ask you one last question, though. Did you recognise the man?"

Amy shook her head and her eyes widened. "If I'd known him I would have asked why he was hiding his prey."

Thank goodness she hadn't. No wonder Alan said she needed looking after. Picking up her phone, Indigo stopped recording and punched in the number of George's mobile, unsure where he would be. He was at the hospital, checking on Spencer-Cooper. She asked him to stay there, saying she had to speak to him about Taylor's car keys. He told her he could wait for half an hour, but had somewhere he needed to be.

She put her phone away and looked down at the young woman, who was watching her silently. "If I was you," she said, "I'd leave these woods. Find somewhere with walls and heating, and food."

"I have food." The voice was quiet and a little sad. "It's just that I sometimes forget to eat."

Oh Amy, she thought as she turned and began to walk away, why isn't somebody looking for you? I wonder if your mother keeps your bed made up and jumps every time the doorbell rings, like the parents who hire me.

Chapter Eighteen

She made her way back to where she'd left the car parked, half on the scrubby verge, got in, fastened her seat belt, and set off for Great Oxing Hospital as fast as she dared. She made it in twenty five minutes and hoped George wouldn't deduce her speed from that. It took her another eight minutes to find the ward where Spencer-Cooper lay. George wasn't in sight, but Lily Spencer-Cooper was. Indigo went up to her.

"I was so sorry to hear about your father. How's he doing?"

The girl's eyes were red with crying, but she smiled for Indigo and said, "He's a bit better. The doctors have stopped talking about survival, now they're talking about brain damage." Tears broke out again and ran down already streaked cheeks.

Indigo fished for the last of her paper hankies and handed it to her. At this rate she was going to have to start carrying a box of them around with her. "I'm sorry," she said again. "I feel so guilty."

Lily scrubbed at her face and shook her head. "Inspector Howard told me you'd asked daddy about his alibi. He lied, didn't he?"

"Lily, it's alright. It doesn't matter."

"I know he lied, because I know where he was that morning."

"You —?" Indigo shook her head in something like disbelief. "You know where he was?"

"He followed me into the woods. He followed me the last three times I saw Alan. He's too big and clumsy to be invisible."

"Oh, Lily."

Lily gave her another brave smile. "I told you what he was like with his daughters and boys, it's compulsive. At least Alan didn't know he was there. I've lost two boyfriends because my father kept lurking around. They thought it was creepy."

She began to understand why Spencer-Cooper had concocted his dodgy alibi. Not only did he not want to be associated with the place where the murder had occurred, but he didn't want to own up to spying on his daughter. "I suppose he followed you back again?"

Lily nodded and Indigo thought once again how lucky the killer had been. Or should that be rash? After all, he killed a man in full view of a public road and parked the murdered man's car in a public car park. He'd been seen by Mrs Hunter and, as she now knew, by Amy Dwyer. If Lily had left the woods five minutes later, she and her father might also have been witnesses.

George Howard appeared around the end of the corridor, carrying two paper cups of liquid. As he got closer she could see it was either tea or coffee. He came up to them and handed the cups to Lily. "I'm not sure what it tastes like," he said in an apologetic tone, "but it's hot and sweet."

"Thank you. Mum really needs this but she won't leave daddy's side."

He accompanied her across to the ward door and held it open for her to enter. Once she was safely inside he came back to Indigo.

"Did she tell you where her father really was?" she asked.

He gave a wry smile and shook his head at the folly. "Yes, stupid man. I can't say I would actually follow my two on a date, but I do understand the urge."

"Ah yes, they're sixteen and thirteen, aren't they? Just getting into boys." She reached out to rub his shoulder, then thought better of it and pulled her hand back. "I'm sure they're sensible girls, George. You don't have anything to worry about."

"You think so?"

She studied him, head on one side. His tone had been light, but she knew how concerned he was with doing the right thing by his daughters. "I might not have children of my own," she said, "but I've dealt with a lot of runaway teenagers. From what you've told me, I'm pretty sure Ellie and Jennie have their heads screwed on right. Divorce can sometimes be a factor in teenage disaffection, but it sounds like you and your ex have handled things well."

"I hope you're right. Since being with you, I've learnt far too much about what can happen to teenagers who lose faith in their parents." Then he shook himself and straightened his shoulders, arranging his face into what she thought of as his official expression. "Now, what was this about the keys?"

It was time to return to business. "I went back to re-interview Amy Dwyer," she said. "I'll explain why in a moment, but while I was talking to her I realised something about those keys. I assume they were Taylor's, by the way?"

"Yes, they belonged to his Honda."

"Okay. The killer loaded Taylor's body into his own car. He stopped further down the road, dumped the body near the protest camp, then got into the car and drove to the Aldgate car park."

"I know all that."

She tutted to indicate that she'd only been setting the scene. "So when did he drop the keys near the sign post? Before he used them to drive to the car park? Which is impossible. Or did he walk back to the woods especially to leave them there?"

He stared at her with his mouth slightly agape. "Oh, my giddy aunt. Why on earth didn't I see that before? There's no way Spencer-Cooper or anyone else could have just strolled out of the woods and tossed the car keys into the weeds. It doesn't fit the known facts. Whatever the killer did when he left Taylor's car at Aldgate, he must have taken the keys with him."

"Probably put them in his pocket without thinking," she agreed. "And I think I know why." She pulled out her phone. "I want you to listen to my interview with Amy. Please have patience. I know it sounds wacky, but just listen to what she's actually saying."

He did as she asked, listening carefully without interruption. When it had come to an end he raised an eyebrow. "You know you can't take her into court, don't you? She's a drug user. The prosecution would make mincemeat out of her."

"I know." She chuckled and met his eyes. "Though part of me would love to see the jury cope with the spider monster. No, we can't use her testimony, but it does flesh out what happened. And it made me start asking how the killer got to the lay-by and where he went from the car park."

"He couldn't have driven to the lay-by. He'd have had to leave his car behind when he took Taylor's."

"But he could have driven to the Aldgate car park."

Howard nodded and pursed his lips as he thought. "Left his car there, you mean, and walked to the lay-by?"

"It's a long way. He might have jogged, or got the bus and jogged the last bit. That black get up he was wearing could pass for running clothes."

"It's possible. And I see where you're going with the keys. If he was transferring from Taylor's car to his own, he could easily have slipped the Honda keys into his pocket when he reached in to get his own. What are you going to do about it?"

This must be that thin line he'd spoken of. He couldn't chase down the clue of the killer's car, because their suspect, Alan, didn't own a car, and the SIO would want to know why he was going off at a tangent. She vented her frustration with a sigh. "In that case, I'll go and talk to Mrs Hunter again. If he did leave his own car in the car park, it would have been there when she arrived for her doctor's visit."

He gave a little nod of acknowledgement. "So it would. Let's get back to the keys. They did end up at the road sign, so the killer must have gone back there at some point to plant them."

"In order to implicate Ronald Spencer-Cooper. Which means he knows him."

"Which he would, if Spencer-Cooper bribed him. What about the woman? Is she an accomplice?"

Indigo chewed a fingernail. "I don't think so," she said at last. "She sounded like she believed what she was saying. I don't think she even knew the dropped item was a set of car keys."

"I agree, that's the impression I got from the call. But she must know the killer well enough to be prepared to lie for him."

"Lie?"

He gave her a look of disgust. "Come on, Indie, she didn't witness what she said she did."

"Oh. Yes, she did lie, but I don't think it was seen that way. More like doing a favour for someone she believed had seen the incident but didn't want to get involved."

"Well, since we don't know who she is, it doesn't help us find him." There was a brief pause, then he asked cautiously, "What do you think he did with that black bag?"

"He could have taken it away with him, but Maisie asked me earlier why he didn't use the axe to attack Spencer-Cooper."

"Maybe he didn't go to the Country Club meaning to kill him."

"Or maybe he'd disposed of the axe along with the plastic and any other incriminating evidence. I thought he might have buried it in the woods, but Amy's story has me thinking he still had everything in that black bag when he drove away." She gave a frustrated sigh. "Still, it could be anywhere."

"Leave that one with me," he said. "Finding the murder weapon is still a legitimate part of our task on the Taylor case." He glanced at his watch. "Now I really must be going. I've got an ex-greens keeper to interview."

They parted amicably and Indigo made her way out of the building, humming cheerfully.

When she reached the hospital car park she noticed a colourfully dressed young woman with green hair, and a rucksack almost as big as herself, wandering among the cars, staring aimlessly into the front windows. Indigo approached her.

"Amy? What are you doing here?"

A big, beaming smile lit her face. "I heard you say you were coming to the hospital. I wanted to talk to you."

"But how did you get here so fast? You've even had time to pack your things."

"I can be fast," she said, "and a nice man in a black car gave me a lift to the High Street."

"Okay. What can I do for you?"

The smile was replaced by confusion and sadness. The girl had remarkably volatile emotions. She'd seen it before in young people who took drugs. Their brain chemistry was all over the place.

"I wanted to do what you said, but I don't know where to go. I don't have anywhere."

Indigo put a hand on her bony shoulder. "Why don't you go home? You do have parents, don't you?"

The sadness became more pronounced. "They won't want me, I'm the screw up. My sister's the good girl, I just get in trouble." Her eyes became pleading and she gave a deep sigh. "I don't want to be a screw up any more. I don't want to do drugs. It scares me, knowing I saw a murderer and didn't even know it. I don't want anything like that to happen ever again."

Good, she'd reached one of those reality checks where it was possible for a person to reassess their life. And it sounded like her parents were good people. The girl hadn't run away from an abusive home. Perhaps there was hope for Amy Dwyer after all.

"Go home," she said. "Tell your parents what you've just told me. They'll help you. You've heard of the Prodigal Son, haven't you?"

Amy looked blank. "No."

What did they teach young people these days? Well, she'd have to spell it out. "Amy, I spend my working life trying to find young people like you. Their parents come and sit in my office and tell me how much they miss their son or daughter. They blame themselves that their teenager has run away from home. They spend sleepless nights worrying about what's happening to them. I doubt if your parents are any different. I promise they'll welcome you back."

Praying she was right, Indigo opened her bag and took out five twenty-pound notes, all she had, and her business card. She wrote her mobile number on the back of the card, and handed both card and money to Amy. "I don't know where you live, but this should pay your fare home. Give your parents one more chance. Tell them you want to quit drugs. When you're ready, call me. I do a lot of work with young people. I have contacts in the drug rehabilitation field. I can put you in touch with someone to help you through."

The girl stared at the money. "How do you know I won't just buy drugs with this?"

"You won't. You're too scared at the moment. Go home before being scared wears off."

Amy dug into the drapes of her skirt and pulled out a purse. Carefully folding the notes and the card, she squashed them into the purse and put it back into her pocket. Then she flung her arms about Indigo's neck and said thank you.

Indigo hugged her, feeling the sparrow-like bones beneath their inadequate covering of skin. Then she stepped back and said, "Come on, I'll give you a lift to the station."

Amy prattled happily on the short drive to Great Oxing railway station and hugged her benefactor once more before going off to buy her ticket. Indigo watched her disappear into the ticket hall with mixed feelings. Oh Amy, she thought, don't blow it. I think this might be your last chance. Then she shook herself out of the threatening gloom of her thoughts and called Mrs Hunter. The woman asked how she was doing and agreed to grant her a second interview.

Chapter Nineteen

As she drove towards the little house she smiled to herself, thinking how her meetings with the key witness were very much in the nature of an audience granted by the elderly woman. She hoped Dawson and the barrister were never put in the position of having to portray Mrs Hunter as a confused old woman, because they would fail miserably.

The door was opened promptly to her ring and the woman in question, arrayed today in a smart pair of black slacks with a crisp white blouse, ushered her once more into the tidy front room.

"Well," said Mrs Hunter, when they were both seated, "I don't know what more I can tell you. I only caught a brief glimpse of the killer, you know, and I wasn't paying too much attention to his face." She waved at the tray on the coffee table. "I made the tea in advance this time. Shall I pour?"

"Yes, please. It's just what I need. All I've had today is one cup of coffee and that was around six this morning."

The woman laughed, a hearty sports mistress kind of laugh. "Oh yes, I remember those days. Too much to do, no time to stop, and you look up at nine o'clock to realise it's night time and you haven't eaten all day." She sounded wistful as she poured two steaming cups of strong tea.

"What work did you do?"

"I was Executive Secretary to the CEO of a medium sized manufacturing company. I had quite a bit of power in my day, though you wouldn't think it to look at me now." She handed Indigo a perilously full cup of tea and glanced around the little room. "I could afford a bigger place, but it would only mean more rooms to clean." She settled back and took a long sip out of her own cup. "Now, tell me what else I can tell you about that wretched man."

"Actually," said Indigo, hurriedly swallowing a mouthful of hot tea, "it's not him I want to talk about. Inspector Howard and I have been talking, and we have a theory. We think the killer may have parked his own car in the car park while he went off to commit the crime."

A glint entered the older woman's eyes. "And you wonder if I saw it?"

My she really was quick. Indigo couldn't see either barrister casting this particular elderly lady as blind or stupid when she finally ended up in court. "Did you?"

"Now you come to mention it, there was another car parked there when I drove in. I noticed it particularly because it was parked right over in the furthest bay. You don't drive over to the furthest bay when the rest of the car park is empty, do you?"

"Not usually. Was it still there when you left?"

"Oh yes."

"Can you describe it?"

"It was a silver Peugeot, dear, I recognised the badge. It was an older model. I could tell you which one if I could see some pictures." She hesitated. "My mobile's in the other room. If you have yours with you perhaps you could do an internet search."

Indigo nodded and slipped her phone from her pocket. She started on the search, then saw the impatient way the older woman was looking at her and handed the phone over. "Here, why don't you look yourself. It'll be quicker."

As Mrs Hunter tapped the screen and scrolled through windows, Indigo sat and watched her, thinking what a shame it was that older people were consigned to some kind of limbo by society. More and more of today's elderly were fit, healthy, well-educated and bored to distraction. That bright, ferocious mind should still be engaged in meaningful activity of some kind, not confined to a small house rereading murder mysteries. A fleeting picture of Taylor's well-ordered but lonely flat flashed through her thoughts and she shivered. What if that was the way her own life was leading? What would she do when she was too old to work?

"This is the one," exclaimed Mrs Hunter, interrupting her melancholy. "That's exactly the same car that was in the car park."

Indigo leant forward and studied the picture on the screen. "Peugeot 207 CC," she read. "Are you absolutely sure?"

"Absolutely. It was definitely a cabriolet. I remember thinking how nice it would be to have a car with a retracting roof. But totally impractical, of course."

She took the phone back and slipped it into her pocket, raising her eyebrows at the look of enquiry on the woman's face.

"You aren't recording this time."

Indigo chuckled. "Not this time. I'll write it up when I get back to the office. I know I can rely on you not to deny anything you've said."

Mrs Hunter inclined her head graciously. "I'll take that as a compliment. Now, is there anything else I can help with?"

"I don't think so. If anything comes up, I'll call, but you've been remarkably helpful already."

"Ah, but has it been of any use to your defence of the youth they imprisoned?"

Indigo stood up and held out her hand. "Very much so. I've got enough to blow their case against Alan out of the water, and Inspector Howard is closing in on the real culprit. Now we know what he drives, well —"

Mrs Hunter rose, shook the proffered hand and led the way to the front door, remaining on the step as Indigo got into her car and drove away.

She felt a certain amount of trepidation as she left, and was glad to see the woman had gone back indoors when she glanced into her rear view mirror at the end of the street. It had just occurred to her that Mrs Hunter was a potential target. The killer couldn't have heard there was a witness, a witness who could pick him out in a line up. She hoped it would stay that way until the police had him safely behind bars, because it had been far too easy to identify her and find out where she lived.

She'd driven away from Mrs Hunter's undecided about what to do next. She wanted to speak to Mrs Barnes again, but she also wanted to get Rupert tracking down silver Peugeots. Driving unconsciously while she dithered, she found herself turning into St Michael's Road, the shopping street where her agency was situated. Well, that settled that problem. She parked in her usual place, hurried around the block and took the stairs at a jog.

Maisie looked up from her terminal as she entered. "You're back then?"

"Only briefly. Is Rupert in?"

"He's in the big office."

The big office was, in fact, slightly smaller than Maisie's reception area, but contained two desks and associated office furniture. This was the base for her two investigators, Rupert Gray and Jack Robins, the latter being currently on site with a commercial client in the Midlands. Rupert was typing up a report on his computer and simultaneously listening to music on his iPod. Indigo didn't know how he could do that, it would spoil her concentration. At the moment it meant she had to physically walk across the room and tap him on the shoulder to get his attention.

He looked up and pulled the ear bud out of one ear. "Oh, hi boss."

"Rupert, I have a job for you."

He nodded and took a notebook from the top drawer of his desk. "Fire away," he said.

"Okay. It looks like the killer could have been driving a silver Peugeot 207 CC on the morning of the murder. I want you to check all our suspects and see if any of them have access to a car like that. Don't just check what they normally drive. The car could belong to a wife or partner."

"Define suspect," he said.

"Let's start with everyone on the board."

"You wiped the board," he reminded her with a hint of reproof in his tone.

"Sorry, I was feeling down. You heard about Ronald Spencer-Cooper?"

"Maisie told me. It's alright, I copied the grid into a spreadsheet anyway. I suppose you want me to omit Amy, Alan and Spencer-Cooper?"

"Omit Amy. I've just discovered she came across the killer as he was hiding the body."

"Wow, another witness."

"A witness who was so high she thought she was watching a giant spider," she told him, with raised eyebrows. "Even so, she gave us valuable information."

"Keep Alan Sherman and Ronald Spencer-Cooper?" He sounded doubtful.

"For the sake of completeness, yes. I don't want to make any assumptions on this case. I've already led myself astray once. Also, add all the other members of the ODC Planning Committee to that list. They didn't vote on the route change, but they might have had influence with Councillor Porter."

"Just the male members?"

She shook her head. "All of them. There's a woman involved in this somehow. Maybe a female member got her husband to do the dirty work for her."

"In that case, do you want me to add Eleanor Knight?"

"Do you know, I hadn't thought of her. Yes, put her down."

Rupert studied her, head on one side. "What if the killer hired the car?" he said.

"We'll look into that if you come up empty on the ownership front."

"What are you going to be doing?"

"Let's just say I'm going to follow a hunch."

His eyes suddenly sparkled with excitement, betraying a touching belief in her ability to solve any case through sheer gut feeling. Maisie had once revealed that he thought Indigo could sense a trail like a big cat. "Anything you want to share?"

"The attack on Spencer-Cooper was less ferocious than the one on Taylor. No, let's put that the other way round. Taylor was attacked with a lot more ferocity than Spencer-Cooper. His head was virtually pulped, I've read the autopsy report."

"That doesn't sound very helpful. I mean, we already knew that." His disappointment was intense. He'd expected her to produce some complicated piece of deductive logic and she'd failed him.

She smiled at the naivety, knowing he'd eventually learn to rely more on routine digging than blinding flashes of intuitive genius. "We may have already known it, but we hadn't asked ourselves what it meant," she said. "They call it overkill. I think the killer had a real hatred for Taylor, the sort of hatred that takes more than a few weeks to develop. I'm not saying the corruption angle doesn't come into it somewhere, maybe it was the final trigger, but I'm convinced those two had a history. I read through the interview transcripts this morning. Eleanor Knight told me Taylor knew someone on the Planning Committee and mistrusted them. Mrs Barnes told me about a run in Taylor had with someone about six years ago. I think there's a chance they were talking about the same person."

"That's a bit of a stretch, isn't it?"

"Maybe, but it's easily checked. Mrs Barnes seems to have been Peter Taylor's only confidante, he must have mentioned the man's name to her at some point. If I can get her to tell me that name, I can match it against the members of the Planning Committee. Either it will match one of them or it won't. There's nothing to lose."

Rupert gave a resigned shrug. "I guess not." He removed the other ear bud and locked his IPod away in a drawer, ready to follow her orders. She chuckled to herself at his downbeat expression, knowing he'd bounce back the moment he started his research, and went into her own office. She'd decided to phone Mrs Barnes this time instead of just turning up on her doorstep. Now she had to work out how to persuade her to talk to the enemy again.

In the event it didn't turn out to be as difficult as she'd expected. She began by telling her about the attack on Ronald Spencer-Cooper and let her know Inspector Howard believed it to be the work of Peter Taylor's killer. She may have implied this was the official view of the police, but was careful not to actually say so. In any case, once Mrs Barnes had conceded Alan Sherman might not be the murderer she became a lot more amenable. Indigo then explained to her she might actually hold the key to the whole mystery, which intrigued her greatly. However Mrs Barnes was just about to go out. She suggested Indigo should call round at seven o'clock and she would tell her what she knew. Indigo agreed and put the phone down.

She now had nearly six hours to spare before her meeting with Mrs Barnes. It would take her one and a half hours to drive to Redhill, which left four and a half hours to fill. She decided to put the case out of her mind for a while and catch up on some of the other work she'd put to one side while she'd been concentrating on getting her nephew out of prison. At four o'clock she packed up and left the office, heading for home. Midnight was nowhere to be seen, so she simply changed her water, put down a bowl of food, grabbed a quick meal for herself, and set off for Redhill promptly at five thirty.

Chapter Twenty

Just after seven o'clock that evening Mrs Barnes opened the door and ushered her into flat number 1, with Abercrombie running around her ankles growling at the scent of cat on her jeans. Her first thought was of how uncomfortable Peter Taylor must have been entering this apartment. It was crammed with possessions; knick-knacks, magazines, cushions, embroidered runners. Nothing was out of place or haphazard, but the overall picture was chaotic and a little claustrophobic, far removed from the neat precision of the apartment upstairs.

Mrs Barnes waved her to an overly plump green velour sofa. "So what is this key piece of information I have, then?"

Indigo got straight to the point. "When I was here last time you mentioned what you called a 'spat' Mr Taylor had had with a young man about six years ago."

"That's right. It set the managers against him."

"Yes, so you said. Could you tell me exactly what happened? Who was this young man?"

"He was one of Peter's staff." The woman settled herself comfortably in a matching green easy chair and leant forward. Her expression suggested she was going to enjoy this chance to gossip about her late friend. "Peter didn't like him right from the first day. Arrogant, he called him, said he was on the make – going drinking with the senior staff, flattering them. He said if this young man had put as much effort into his work as he did into networking with the directors he might have been a halfway decent planner. As it was, poor Peter was always having to be on his tail to get jobs done right."

A member of staff? The transcript of the previous interview had hinted as much, but she'd been holding out the hope Taylor's nemesis had actually been a councillor. Still, an ex local government officer might decide to stand for political office himself. After all, he'd know the way the system worked, and it sounded as if this mystery man was good at gaining supporters. Not Bill Porter, though, he'd always worked at the plastics factory. One of the other members of the planning committee, then?

"So, was there any particular incident that caused the managers to turn against Mr Taylor or was it just the antipathy between him and this young man?"

"Oh, there was an incident alright." Her lips compressed into a line of disapproval. "It seems people in local government can't just get promoted like normal folk. If they want a better job they have to wait for one to be advertised and then apply for it. Sounds silly to me, but Peter said there are ways of getting round it, reorganisations and acting up and things."

"Acting up? That sounds like somebody behaving badly," said Indigo, puzzled.

For the first time something like amusement crossed Mrs Barnes' features. "It does, doesn't it? Peter had to explain it to me too. He said you can ask someone to act at a higher grade and pay them for that grade, but it's only temporary. Anyway, Peter wouldn't have asked this young man to act at a higher grade because he didn't think much of him. So, when the young man applied for a better job in another department and Peter was asked what he thought of him, he told the truth."

"Oh dear, you mean he gave him a negative reference?"

"That's what the managers called it later when they told Peter off, but he said he was entitled to warn the other manager about the young man's work ethic. Well, of course, the young man didn't get the job and he found out Peter had been the reason. He stormed into his office and screamed abuse at him. Peter said he was quite frightened, but he stood his ground. He put him on what he called a disciplinary. I gathered that was some kind of official telling off that would go on his record and affect his future.

"That's when the young man called in favours. Peter found himself in front of some of the directors and they said he shouldn't have given this negative reference. They said the young man was entitled to feel aggrieved and the disciplinary looked like pure spite."

"How did Mr Taylor react to that?"

"He was very upset. He was never a spiteful man. A bit of a stickler for protocol maybe, but he did have to maintain discipline. The directors forced him to withdraw the disciplinary and Peter felt they'd undermined his authority. He said his staff wouldn't take any notice of him in future if he couldn't punish them when they stepped out of line."

"I see. What happened to the young man? Surely he didn't carry on working for Mr Taylor after all that?"

"Oh no, he got a better job in another council. Peter said his friends set it up for him. That's when things started going badly for Peter, and eventually they made him redundant."

"What do you think would have happened if Peter had come across this young man again? Do you think he'd have sought revenge?"

"Oh, Peter wasn't the vengeful type. No, he'd have tried to avoid him, I suppose. Peter could be very cold towards anyone who upset him."

"What if he suspected this young man had done something illegal? What would he have done then?"

"He'd report him, no question, and he'd have enjoyed doing it too. Peter wasn't a saint. He'd have felt satisfaction at being right about him all along." Her eyes narrowed shrewdly. "Is he the one you think killed him?"

"Possibly. It sounds like there was a lot of bad blood between them." She'd concentrated on the councillors because they were the ones who made the decisions, but now she began to wonder who'd asked for the route change in the first place, and a suspicion was forming in her mind. She took a deep breath and asked the vital question. "Mrs Barnes you keep referring to him as the young man. Don't you know his name?"

"Peter called him by his surname and I've been trying and trying to remember it. I just keep thinking about that old film. You know, the one about the boy who stole a postal order."

"An old film?" asked Indigo, wondering why the conversation had suddenly taken such an odd turn.

"An old black and white film. It's got something to do with the name, I'm sure it has."

Indigo had a brainwave. Earlier she'd used an internet search to identify the silver car. What if she tried to identify the film Mrs Barnes was talking about? It might be enough to jog her memory and retrieve the name. She picked up her phone and flicked to internet mode. "Well then, let's see if we can find that film, shall we?"

It took her a few moments to think of a suitable keyword phrase, then she typed in 'film boy steals postal order'. Within seconds she had a list of sites, with the same film title prominently displayed in all of them. She stared at them in triumph as her suspicion crystallised. Turning the screen towards Mrs Barnes she said, "Is this what you were trying to remember?"

The woman peered at the tiny screen with her eyes scrunched. "The Winslow Boy," she read. "Yes, that's right. Peter called him Winslow. I don't know his first name though."

"Don't worry," said Indigo as she put the phone back in her pocket. "I do."

Driving back through the Autumn dark Indigo kept saying to herself 'Winslow, Derian Winslow, who would have thought it?' She hadn't liked him, in fact he'd irritated the life out of her, but she'd never have considered him capable of such a vicious murder. He was simply an annoying poseur, a patronising chauvinist. She could see he and Taylor would have rubbed against each other given their personalities, but murder?

She thought about the story Mrs Barnes had told her. Peter Taylor had blamed Winslow for the perceived decline of his career after their clash, but how had Derian Winslow felt about the incident? After all, it'd been Winslow who'd lost a good job through Taylor's intervention. From what little she knew of the man, she didn't think that would have gone down well. He was one of those irritating people with complete and absolute belief in their own superiority. Taylor was the little man who'd dared to get in his way. Would Winslow have wanted to punish him? Maybe he had actively turned people against Taylor to get revenge.

What if Taylor had threatened him again? That brought her back to the problem of corruption. She'd only considered the members of the planning committee when thinking about the people Spencer-Cooper might have bribed, but why not Winslow? After all, it had to be him who'd written the report recommending the change of route. Looked at from that angle, Derian Winslow was a key person for Ronald Spencer-Cooper to influence. The one reservation she had was that Winslow wasn't the type to do favours for anyone unless it promoted his own goals. What could the country club owner have offered him to make him risk the glittering future he saw for himself?

She brought her thoughts back to the question of what Winslow would have done if confronted by Taylor and decided to work on the hypothesis he had, in fact, accepted a bribe. Taylor's threat of exposure would have dragged up all the memories of that lost job and the disciplinary, persuading Winslow the other was a danger to him. In which case, he might well have decided to eliminate the threat by eliminating the person making it.

She suddenly saw how Winslow's personality fitted the strange combination of forethought and rashness evident in the crime. The killer had thought out certain aspects of his plan; the plastic sheeting, the rubbish bag, the handy suspects in the protest camp. Yet he'd committed the murder on a public road and swapped cars in a public car park. Winslow would have planned, certain his intelligence could outsmart the police, but his belief in his own invincibility would also have made him reckless in seeing the plan through.

But what of the attack on Spencer-Cooper? Just tidying up loose ends, or had he started to weaken, threatening to give the game away?

She caught herself in a yawn. This was making her head ache and she decided to put it out of her mind until the morning. All she'd proved so far was that Peter Taylor and Derian Winslow were old enemies. That wasn't going to free Alan. Tomorrow she'd go over the evidence and see if a case could be built. There were still one or two questions she wanted to follow up from her previous interviews.

She switched on the radio and tried to concentrate on a current affairs programme, but her stomach muscles were knotted with excitement. She was closing in, she knew she was. It was exactly the same feeling she had when she picked up a runaway's scent.

Chapter Twenty One

Indigo had had a long and tiring day and had fallen into bed almost as soon as she got home. Consequently she forgot to set the alarm clock and was only woken by the sound of Midnight scratching at her bedroom door for food. Despite rushing about the house like a demented thing, forgetting about breakfast for herself and presenting the cat with the first sachet of cat food that came to hand, it was nine thirty by the time she got into the office.

Maisie was seated at her desk, typing sporadically at her computer keyboard, and Rupert was lounging comfortably in a chair beside it. They'd been talking, but stopped when Indigo entered and turned to give her startled looks.

She flapped her hands in their direction. "Okay, okay, I'm late. It doesn't happen that often, so there's no need to make a big deal of it."

"We're not," said Maisie, her face breaking into a wide grin. "But Indie, pet, do you know your hair's sticking up on end?"

Indigo clapped a hand to her head and realised Maisie was telling the truth. "Oh damn," she said. "I forgot to brush it. The alarm didn't go off. The cat woke me up, scratching for food." She stopped, took three deep breaths, then said calmly. "I'm just going to sort myself out. Stay here, you two, I have news."

"You know, for someone who didn't want a pet, you've really taken to that animal, haven't you?" Maisie called after her as she disappeared down the passage that led to the toilet and kitchen. She took the time to sort out her hair, put on her make up, and make a mug of coffee. When she got back, her two employees were still as she'd left them. Only now they were watching her expectantly.

She stood in the middle of the office and turned her eyes to the young man. "Any luck finding that car I set you on?"

He gave a triumphant grin. "Actually, yes. One of our suspects drives just that make, model and colour. You'll never guess who."

"Derian Winslow."

His face collapsed into a scowl. "I hate it when you do that."

"Sorry." She threw him a look of sympathy. "I didn't mean to steal your thunder, but Mrs Barnes identified Winslow as the young man Taylor fell out with when he worked in local government." She frowned, suddenly feeling much less sure of herself. "To be more accurate, she identified the surname Winslow. I've just assumed she meant Derian."

"He is a local government bloke," said Maisie reassuringly. "I'd say it was a reasonable guess. "

Indigo nodded and proceeded to tell them all she'd learnt the previous day, concluding with her thoughts on the way home. "Now we know Winslow drives the type of car Mrs Hunter saw in the car park, it's beginning to look bad for him. He said he was driving his partner to work at the time of the murder. I'll have to find out who she is and where she works."

"Carol Enfield," said Rupert quickly. "She lives with Winslow in Nunsfield and she's employed as a designer with Forster and Partners. It's a small firm of architects, situated near Aldgate."

"That's very good, Rupert. I'm always impressed by how thorough you are." He flushed with pleasure, but she carried on as if she hadn't noticed, knowing he hated looking so unsophisticated around her. "So, he could have dropped her at work and then turned round and left the car in the car park, before going back to meet Taylor at the lay-by."

"I wonder if she was the sheila who called in the tip about Spencer-Cooper," said Maisie.

Indigo smiled at the lapse into Aussie slang. Her friend tried hard to keep her speech professional, but native colloquialisms had a way of slipping in from time to time. She nodded. "That's what I was thinking. If they drove past the woods earlier that morning, as Winslow claimed, it would be easy for him to persuade her he'd seen Spencer-Cooper. Coming in to Great Oxing the driver's side would be closest to the woods, so he'd have had a better view than her."

"But how would he explain not reporting it himself?" asked Rupert, his brow furrowed.

Indigo chuckled and shook her head as an image of Winslow entered her mind. "If you'd met him, you wouldn't ask that. He probably implied it was beneath his dignity as a senior council executive. Or that his acquaintanceship with Spencer-Cooper made it improper for him to be the one to report the incident."

"I don't think I'd want to meet him," said Maisie. "I thought he sounded condescending when I transcribed your interview with him." She rubbed at her chin. "So, do you want me to get everything ready for you to pass to the police?"

Indigo shook her head. "Not yet. We don't have enough to convince them."

"Oh, come on."

"We don't, Maisie. My case against Spencer-Cooper was tighter than this. At the moment I don't even have the kind of circumstantial evidence Chief Inspector Waters used to put Alan in jail. No, I've got to get something more substantial."

"Well I don't see what more you can do unless you twist his arm and make him confess."

"Don't be silly, I still have leads to follow."

"I see. Then you're either trying to impress that police inspector of yours or you're trying to prove him wrong."

Indigo glared at her, causing Rupert to jump up and edge towards the corridor. "If you must know, George is now convinced of Alan's innocence. It's his SIO we've got to prove things to."

Maisie's eyes narrowed. "If he's on your side now, does that mean you're a couple again?"

That was a loaded question and one she couldn't answer. They appeared to be working together, but there was still this invisible gap between them. She shook her head. "I don't think so. Maybe he just needed an excuse to break up. It doesn't matter right now. Alan's the important thing."

"Oh Indie, I'm sorry. You really care for him, don't you?"

Ignoring the question, Indigo followed Rupert and asked him to write down the address of Forster and Partners for her. She planned to see Carol Enfield and find out if she had indeed made the phone call accusing Spencer-Cooper. When she passed through the reception area on her way out Maisie was deliberately concentrating on her screen, as if trying not to stir her emotions. As she went down the stairs, Indigo felt a heaviness in her chest. What if the break up was permanent? What if George asked whether they could stay friends? She felt a prickle in her eyelids and shook her head angrily. She should concentrate on her task. There would be time to worry about her love life once Alan was free.

She hadn't called Carol Enfield to make an appointment because she was hoping to trade on the shock value of her sudden appearance. Instead, she found the address Rupert had given her and parked in the large car park adjacent to the office block. The building itself was an old one, let out by the floor. A board on the left hand wall of the lobby showed that Forster and Partners occupied the whole of the first floor. There was no reception desk, but a uniformed security man sat in a little cubicle next to the lift. When she approached him he asked her name and glanced down a printed list in front of him.

"I don't have an appointment," she said quickly. "I need to speak to Miss Enfield in Forster and Partners rather urgently. Perhaps you could phone through and ask her to let me come up?"

He gave her a disapproving look. "We prefer it if people make appointments in advance," he said. "It makes our job easier." Having put her in her place, however, he looked up Carol Enfield's number on his computer terminal and picked up the phone.

"Could you tell her Indigo Lattimer needs to talk to her about the telephone call she made two days ago? Thank you."

She stood patiently by the cubby hole while the man relayed her message, wondering if Carol would even agree to see her. If she couldn't talk to her here, she'd have to find some other way. The problem was she didn't know what the woman looked like. Otherwise she could wait outside the building and catch her when she went to lunch.

He put the phone down and she looked up expectantly. "Miss Enfield says she'll come down and talk with you."

There was no seating available in the small, tile-floored lobby so Indigo stood where she could watch both the lift door and the staircase that led down from the upper floor. She kept one eye on the clock as well. There was a danger Carol would phone Winslow and ask him what to do and Indigo didn't really want to alert him to her suspicions, given how dangerous and unpredictable he might be. If she spooked him into something even more rash than the attack on Spencer-Cooper, George Howard would never forgive her.

It was a full ten minutes before a woman came down the stairs. She was in her late twenties, with gorgeous auburn hair and a figure to die for. She was elegantly dressed and her make up was perfect. Despite all this, she gave off an air of depression. Her shoulders were slumped, her eyes pointed downwards towards the steps in front of her. When she reached the bottom of the stairs she momentarily glanced round to find Indigo, then dropped her gaze again to the floor. All in all, she looked defeated.

Indigo recognised the symptoms. Her business occasionally brought her into contact with battered wives who had exactly that look of self-loathing and despair. She didn't think for one moment Winslow actually hit his partner, but she suspected he chipped away at her self-esteem at every opportunity. His attitude towards women was very much that of a superior being indulging their frailty. She recalled how inept and clumsy she'd felt in his office. What must it be like living with that on a regular basis? She gave a sigh and wondered why any woman would put up with that, much less a beauty like Carol Enfield.

The woman came over and stood directly in front of her. There was a quick, painful meeting of eyes before she looked down again, leaving Indigo to wonder how she held down a professional job if she couldn't meet people's gaze.

"I don't know anything about a phone call," she said, her voice barely louder than a whisper.

"Look Carol, given the context of that call, I don't think this is the best place for us to talk. Isn't there somewhere else we could go?"

"I didn't make a phone call."

Accepting any conversation they had was going to take place here in the lobby, Indigo launched her attack. "I know it was you who called my PA on the morning of the fourteenth," she said. "You told her you'd seen Ronald Spencer-Cooper come out of Oxley Woods around the time of Peter Taylor's murder and that you also saw him throw something onto the grass verge." Carol Enfield gave a tiny gasp of pain, but Indigo carried on ruthlessly. "I now know you couldn't have seen any of that, because it didn't happen."

The woman looked up and finally met her eyes fully. Her own were filled with fear. She caught hold of Indigo's left wrist. "I don't know anything about that," she said, enunciating each word carefully. "Please go away."

Indigo raised her right hand and covered the cold, shaking hand of the other. "Carol, what we found in the place you directed us to could only have been dropped by the killer. But it wasn't dropped on the morning of the murder, it couldn't have been."

She allowed that to sink in and saw the fear slowly change to terror as understanding came. "I know he told you to call me," she said gently. "I know he frightens you, but if you tell us the truth you'll be free of him. Trust me."

Carol Enfield pulled away and raised her voice. "Please go away, Miss Lattimer. I have nothing further to say to you."

There was a scraping sound from the direction of the cubicle and Indigo glanced at the security man, who was opening the gate and preparing to come towards them. She pulled a business card out of her bag and thrust it into Carol's unresisting hand. "If you change your mind, call me," she said. "He will be caught and you don't want to be treated as an accomplice."

She made for the exit, glancing back as she opened the doors. The security man was talking to Carol and gesturing in Indigo's direction. The woman appeared to reassure him, then started to walk towards the stairs, her gait unsteady. Indigo gave a sigh of frustration and went back to her car. She hadn't anticipated Carol being so scared of Winslow she couldn't see where her best interests lay. She'd allowed for her to be so in love with him she wouldn't believe what she was told, but there was no love there, only fear and abject misery. Either way, it didn't help her get the proof she needed.

Chapter Twenty Two

She sat in the car for a few minutes debating what to do next. Once Winslow was in custody Carol would probably crack and tell all, but before that could happen she needed to build a case strong enough to convince DCI Waters to arrest Winslow and let Alan go. Just one little thing that materially linked Derian Winslow to either Taylor or the lay-by would be enough, given everything else she had.

She pulled out a notebook in which she'd made notes the morning before when she read through the interview transcripts. She looked through them, ticking off the leads she'd already checked. There was one left – Mrs Barnes had told her Taylor didn't like computers and preferred to do things by hand. How was that going to help?

She got out her mobile and called Eleanor Knight, hoping she wasn't in a meeting. She was available and seemed happy to talk. Indigo asked her if the police had taken all Taylor's papers away.

Eleanor sounded confused. "All the paperwork on his desk was hardcopy from the computer. They took all that with them."

"I heard he didn't like using computers."

The other's laugh echoed across the airwaves. "Let's just say that as far as Peter was concerned the computer was a glorified typewriter. He was excellent at Word, he answered emails efficiently and in great detail, but he was barely competent at Excel and couldn't use PowerPoint at all. My pet bugbear was his Outlook Calendar, he never filled it in. You never knew where he was going to be. If you sent him a meeting invitation, he deleted it and didn't bother to reply."

She found this difficult to square with everything she'd learnt about the man. "You surprise me," she said. "I'd have expected him to keep meticulous track of meetings and appointments."

"Maybe he did," said Eleanor. "He always turned up for them and he was always at the right place for the right time. Maybe he kept track some other way, but he turned a deaf ear to my requests to keep his public calendar up to date."

A tingling sensation ran across the back of Indigo's neck. There had been no diary on the body or found in the dead man's car. "Miss Knight," she said, "would you mind me having a look through the desk he used? That's assuming it hasn't been cleared out."

"Nobody's touched it since the police came round. If you think it'll be of help, please do come and take a look. Ask reception to phone through to Janice. I'll tell her to expect you."

Indigo thanked her and closed the call. Every instinct told her to race to Henckle and Green as fast as she could, but she drove at her normal speed and observed every red light on the way. If there was anything to find in Taylor's desk it had been there for over a month and wasn't going to disappear in the next hour.

Henckle and Green's reception area was as shiny, slick and cold as it had been on her previous visits. Thankfully, she didn't have to wait in it for long. Janice must have been hanging round waiting for her to appear, because she came walking out of the lift only moments after the receptionist had called her. She was virtually vibrating with excitement.

"You have a lead, don't you?" she demanded when they were in the lift on their way up. "I knew, when Miss Knight told me you were coming. I mean, you wouldn't come back a third time if you weren't following some lead. Would you?"

"I'm hoping Mr Taylor left something very useful in his desk."

Janice's face fell dramatically. "There's nothing in his desk but stationery. The police asked about personal possessions, but I told them he only had work things in his desk."

They'd reached the Marketing Suite and Indigo followed the young woman out of the lift. "Did they check the desk anyway?" she asked the other's back.

Janice shook her head without turning round. "Not really. I gave them all the files out of his bottom drawer, but they didn't bother with the stationery. I mean, what was the point?"

Indigo caught up with her. "Well, let's go and take a look now, shall we? Just in case."

Janice's demeanour said she thought it would be a waste of time, but she dutifully led the way into the main office and to one of the three empty desks. Indigo recalled there had been two desks empty when she was here last, but now Butterworth's desk stood clear and unused as well. Each desk had a pedestal containing three drawers pushed under the right hand side. She began her search with the bottom drawer. It was a deep, file drawer and held hanging folders for filing papers. They were all empty and there was nothing in the drawer beneath them.

"Like I said, I gave all them papers to the police."

"Just double checking," murmured Indigo.

She opened the middle drawer. It contained spare A4 manila folders, plastic sleeves, a couple of empty display books. She rifled through them. Just stationary, as Janice had said, and all of it arranged in that precise way she'd come to associate with Peter Taylor. She opened the top drawer, her spirits beginning to sink. A pen tray sat on little ridges at the top of the drawer. Indigo looked at it and sighed. Nobody kept their pen tray that tidy, the man was clinical. It didn't even contain any of the odd coins which often found their way into other people's trays. She pushed the tray to the back of the drawer. Beneath it were three sizes of envelope, neatly placed side by side.

She was about to close the drawer and admit defeat when she decided she might as well be thorough and take the pen tray out. She'd probably find more envelopes, but it was as well to check. It wasn't more envelopes. At the back of the drawer, behind the envelopes, was an A5 sized one-day-a-page 2025 desk diary. Indigo took it out and waved it at Janice.

"I thought you said there was only stationery?"

The other looked confused. "But it is stationery. I mean, we've still got half a dozen of them in the stationery cupboard."

Indigo shook her head, but was only mildly surprised. She'd accurately judged the young woman's mental acuity on her first visit. She opened the diary and flipped through, her hand trembling slightly. The pages were blank for the first five months, then in June they began to be filled with small, neat, rather beautiful penmanship. This was the first time she'd seen any of Taylor's handwriting other than the signatures on his drawings and she thought it suited him perfectly.

The entries were all appointments. Taylor had recorded the time of the meeting, the location of the meeting, the person who'd called the meeting, and a brief note about the subject. With her heart beating erratically, she turned to the fifth of August and there it was, right at the top of the page – 9am, lay-by, Winslow, proof not bribed. She stood staring at it for a long couple of minutes. If Janice hadn't misled the police, if they'd ignored her and searched the desk anyway, if any one of a number of things had happened differently, Alan Sherman wouldn't have been charged with murder and Derian Winslow would. What's more, Ronald Spencer-Taylor wouldn't have been attacked.

She carefully put the diary back into the drawer and replaced the pen tray. There was a lock in the top drawer which, Indigo knew, would lock the whole of the pedestal. The key sat in a section of the pen tray. She closed the drawer, locked it and handed the key to Janice.

"Guard that key with your life," she said. "Lock it away somewhere secure and don't give it to anyone but the policeman who comes to ask you for it. Do you understand me?"

Janice nodded her understanding and Indigo had no option but to trust her. "Is that book evidence?"

"Yes, very important evidence. That's why only the police should be allowed to take it away."

The PA frowned at her, eyebrows knitting. "But can't you take it to the police?"

Indigo shook her head patiently. "I'm working for the defence. You can vouch for the fact you were with me when I found the book in the drawer, but if I took it away the prosecution could accuse me of tampering with it."

Janice's eyes widened. "Really?"

"Really."

She was even more tempted to speed when she left Henckle and Green. Common sense told her the desk diary would be safe enough until the police got there, but her nerves wouldn't be happy until it was in their custody. She was well on her way to the incident room at Great Oxing police station when her mobile phone rang.

She never spoke on the phone when she was driving, not even using a hands free device. Consequently, she was inclined to let this go to voice mail. Then it occurred to her that maybe Carol Enfield had changed her mind and was willing to speak to her. She pulled over and parked at the curb, catching the call before the caller rang off. It wasn't Carol, it was George Howard.

"I was just coming to see you," she said.

"Now there's a coincidence. I have some news for you."

"They've released Alan."

His sigh sounded like wind crackling down the phone. "Indie, please. As soon as we've got enough to convince Rick Waters, I'll get him out for you. I promise he won't stay in prison a moment longer than he has to."

"Sorry, what was it you wanted to tell me?"

"I called to let you know we'd found the black rubbish bag."

"That's rather an impressive piece of work. Where was it?'

"Actually, you put me onto it. You remember we talked about the killer having the black bag with him when he reached the Aldgate car park?"

"Amy's testimony, yes."

"Well, I got to thinking. He wouldn't want to carry incriminating evidence around with him for very long, and there's an empty building right next to the car park."

"The place that's boarded up? With the 'To Let' sign?"

"That's the one," he agreed. "We got the owners permission to search it and found the black bag inside. It wasn't the only one. The boarding on the window is loose and the glass is broken. It looks like several people have been using it as an unofficial tip. Lots of rubbish sorting for the SOCO guys, but they found the one we wanted, that's all that matters."

She felt a sudden surge of curiosity. "So, what was in the bag?"

"The plastic sheeting, of course. We knew that was there because Amy saw him put it in. The axe was there too."

"That's why he couldn't use it to attack Spencer-Cooper?"

"Luckily, or he'd almost certainly have killed him. There were also some clothes; a black hooded top and jogging bottoms, black trainers, and black leather driving gloves. They're all with forensics as we speak. They're hoping to get skin flakes from the clothes so we can get some DNA." He paused, then said cautiously, "That might get your nephew out."

"I can do better than that," she said. "I know who the killer is and I have proof."

There was a gasp, which gave her a great sense of satisfaction. George Howard wasn't taken by surprise very often. "You're sure?"

"This time I'm certain. Look, I'm not far away from Great Oxing. I can be at the central police station in about fifteen minutes if you can meet me there. Then I'll explain everything."

She made it in twelve minutes, but he was already waiting to shepherd her up through the back offices to a tiny meeting room, barely big enough to seat four. Although he was so anxious to hear her news that his brows appeared permanently entwined, he made time to ask if she needed something to drink. She glanced at the clock and realised it was lunchtime. "Yes please. All I've had today is one cup of coffee."

He disappeared for a few minutes and came back with two mugs of strong tea, one of which he put in front of her. "Okay," he said as he sat down opposite her. "Let's have it."

She began with Mrs Hunter and the silver car, and left nothing out. When she got to the Winslow Boy he raised an eyebrow but made no comment. Not until she finally told him about the desk diary did he speak.

"Somebody's going to get into trouble over that," he said darkly. "They should have searched those drawers no matter what that girl said." He studied her, then said in a serious tone, "I know you don't like calling yourself a detective, but you've got a detective's instincts. I'd have you on my squad any day."

"Why, thank you George," she answered primly. Then she leant forward and put her hand over his. "What are you going to do now? Will this be enough for DCI Waters, or do I have to catch Winslow standing over a body with an axe in his hand?"

He smoothed her fingers absent-mindedly. "The first thing is to get someone over to Henckle and Green to secure that diary. Then I shall personally go and ask Mr Derian Winslow to accompany me back here for a little chat. I expect he'll be at the Civic Centre at this time on a Friday."

"Hadn't you better let Waters arrest him?" she asked, only half joking.

A twinkle entered his eyes. "Unfortunately, the DCI is on a training course today. He's a great believer in keeping abreast of the latest business techniques, is our Rick."

"I see." She removed her hand from his and stood up. "You will get Alan out as soon as you can, won't you? Like you said."

"I'll put the wheels in motion as soon as Winslow's been formally charged." He accompanied her to the door. "You won't mind if I get someone else to see you out of the building?" His face broke into a grin. "I have some urgent business to attend to."

She met his gaze and grinned back. "I quite understand, Inspector."

Chapter Twenty Three

She'd meant to go straight back to the agency after leaving the police station, but when she got to her car it occurred to her Carol Enfield might have had time to change her mind about talking to her. She wouldn't mention the imminent arrest of Carol's partner, just call and ask if she'd had second thoughts. In truth, she felt sorry for the woman and wanted to give her a last chance to do the right thing. As it stood there was a real risk Carol could be charged with perverting the course of justice or even of being an accomplice.

The efficient Rupert had supplied Carol's work phone number along with the address, so Indigo sat in her car outside the police station and dialled it. The phone rang for quite a while, but she could be extremely patient when she wanted. Eventually it was answered and a harassed voice said, "Miss Enfield's phone."

"Oh." It hadn't occurred to her Carol wouldn't be there. "Is Miss Enfield about?"

"She's gone home." The voice betrayed even more stress. "She went off sick about half an hour ago, looking all white and trembling. If you want her she might be back on Monday. I've got enough to do with my own work, without answering her damn phone every few minutes. I just hope I haven't picked up whatever she's got."

"I hope not – " The phone at the other end was slammed down, cutting off her words of sympathy.

Indigo thought it likely Carol's apparent sickness had been caused by their earlier conversation. She'd more or less told the woman Winslow was a killer and Carol had already been frightened of him. What would she do once she knew the truth? She didn't have to think about that for very long. Run, of course. Carol Enfield had gone home to pack.

Putting her mobile on the passenger seat, she started her engine. She couldn't let her disappear at this point in the action. As she'd pointed out to Alan, there are times when running away is an automatic confession of guilt. If Carol was going to come over as the innocent dupe Indigo believed her to be, she was going to have to stay put and tell the police everything she knew.

She drove to Nunsfield on automatic pilot, her mind going over the case and looking at her interviews in light of what she now knew. There were still questions, of course. Not least being the matter of corruption. Did Ronald Spencer-Cooper bribe various people to save his club? If so, who and how? The police would have to delve into that aspect, and Spencer-Cooper himself would have to be questioned. Assuming he survived without serious brain damage.

When she reached the outskirts of Nunsfield she punched Winslow's address into her GPS unit. Although it was quite a small town, and one she was familiar with, she didn't know every street. The house she sought was in a new executive development built on what had previously been farm land. She followed the directions carefully and eventually found herself driving down a road lined with painfully new, blandly expensive houses. Not her cup of tea at all. Still it was the sort of place Winslow would see as a stepping stone on his way to that country mansion he no doubt envisioned as his natural home.

She laughed at herself and turned right into Acorn Crescent, the street where Winslow lived. She spotted the house straight away, mainly because there was a silver Peugeot 207 CC parked at an absurd angle across the pavement, it's front wheels barely on the owner's driveway. The driver's door was wide open, making her heart jump. Not only was Winslow home, but he was in a tearing hurry to achieve something. She parked blocking the drive of the next door house and got out. Cautiously, she approached number 17, skirting the silver car.

It wasn't until she'd got beyond both the Peugeot and the blue Ford parked neatly in front of it that she saw the front door also stood wide open. This was where the American PI would take out his gun and confront the villain. Not having a gun, her best choice was to call George and let him know where his quarry was. Only she'd left her mobile in the car. She cursed herself, and had half-turned to go back when a very definite scream reached her from inside the house. She hesitated, the man had killed one person and attempted to kill another, there wasn't time to call the police. Even going back to her car would waste precious seconds. She ran into the house.

Once in the hall she had a better idea of what was going on. From somewhere upstairs came the sound of hammering. Someone was hitting something wooden with a heavy object. A man was muttering and grunting, but she couldn't make out any words, only the intense anger that lay behind them. A woman's voice, slightly muffled by some barrier, alternated between screams and pleading for Derian to stop. She decided Carol had locked herself in one of the bedrooms and Winslow was trying to batter his way in. She had no doubts as to what he would be battering once he got access to the woman.

Shielded by the commotion going on above her, she crept up the stairs until she stood at the top landing. Before her was a short corridor with a door at the end and two in each side wall. Winslow was outside the far door, pounding at it with a sturdy hammer. He'd already managed to break a hole in one of the panels and appeared to be trying to destroy it completely.

Indigo took a few more steps towards him, not wanting to be right on the edge of the stairs for their confrontation. Then she cleared her throat and spoke loudly.

"It's all over Winslow. The police are on their way right now. Why don't you put down the hammer and give up?"

He spun in a one eighty degree arc to face her. For a moment she wondered if he took drugs. She'd never seen eyes that wild on anyone sober, but the wildness quickly faded when he saw her. He hefted the hammer, realigning the position of his hands to make it a better weapon.

"It's not over until I decide it's over," he said.

She felt a shiver run through her body. His tone was that of a manager exerting control over a rowdy meeting. She replied with calm rationality, hoping to convince him of the hopelessness of his position. "We can prove you killed Peter Taylor. The police have the black bag you dumped in the empty shop."

He smiled and gave a shrug of dismissal, meeting her eyes calmly. "They can't link it to me, I bought everything new."

Oh boy, she thought, have you lost it. "But you'll have left DNA on everything, and it will be stained with Taylor's blood. Put the hammer down, hey? Let's be civilised about this."

He looked at the hammer, then back to her. "I'm not going to let you ruin my plans. I'm not going to let any of you ruin my plans."

"Is that what Taylor did? Did he threaten your career again?"

Pure hatred flared momentarily in his eyes. "I wasn't going to let him destroy me. He tried it once before, but he didn't succeed that time either."

"Derian, the only person who's –"

"Oh, this is annoying."

She had only a second to note the change of inflection and prepare for the assault, but her body was trained by years of practice. As he ran at her, with the hammer above his head ready to bring down on hers, she stepped to one side. Catching his right wrist with her left hand and his upper arm with her right hand, she swung herself around so his arm came across her right shoulder and his right hip met hers. Using his own forward momentum, she pulled him across her body and flipped him so he spun round and landed on his back, the hammer skittering away down the stairs.

She'd tried to flip him so he landed on the floor rather than plummeting down the stairs. After all, she didn't want to kill the man. For a moment he did come to rest on the edge of the stairs, winded and gasping for breath. Then he struggled to rise and the movement unbalanced him. He slid forwards and down, shouting and swearing as he hit the treads.

The noise must have muffled the sound of people arriving in the hallway below because, when she stepped forward to check he was alright, she was surprised to see George Howard standing in the doorway with Winslow sprawled out at his feet.

He looked up and met her eyes, his expression that of the imperturbable policeman, but the brown eyes dancing with laughter. "Ah, Indie. You got here before me, then?"

After that it was all confusion. George occupied himself with the arrest of Derian Winslow. To be sure his prisoner was okay, and to avoid any legal difficulties in the future, he sent him off to hospital to be checked over, with a constable riding in the ambulance and another one detailed to meet them there.

In the meantime Indigo took it upon herself to coax Carol Enfield from the master bedroom, where she'd been barricaded against Winslow's murderous assault. It took a while to persuade her she was safe. Only when she was assured Winslow had left the premises would she open the door and come out. Then she collapsed onto Indigo's chest and wept hysterically. In the end she too was bundled off to hospital for a medical once over. As the whole crime scene palaver began, Indigo decided to slip out and make her way home.

Before she left she asked George one question. "That was a very fortuitous arrival. How did you come to be here? I thought you were going to the Civic Centre.'

"Not without checking he was there, obviously. I called his PA and asked."

"And she told you he'd gone home?"

"She told me he'd left in a raging hurry, ignoring an important meeting. I knew something was up, so I thought I'd better get here quick to find out what." His eyes narrowed in suspicion. "I'm not going to ask what you're doing here. Still, I'm glad you were, I wouldn't have enjoyed adding Carol Enfield to his list of victims."

She put a hand on his arm. "I phoned to see if she'd reconsider talking to me. When I heard she'd gone off sick, I knew she was going to run. I couldn't let her do that, could I?"

Someone called to him and he waved a hand in acknowledgement. "You look like you're about to disappear," he told her, "and I need to take another formal statement from you. Two formal statements from you, come to that." He pursed his lips, glanced at the open door, then at the bustling police, then back at Indigo. "Go on then. I'll take them tomorrow afternoon at the incident room." Then he turned and walked away.

Chapter Twenty Four

It was forty-eight hours before Alan Sherman walked to freedom through the gates of Lewes Prison. His parents were waiting for him and whisked him away to be reunited with his siblings, but Indigo didn't get to visit until the following afternoon. He seemed subdued, his face marked by scabbed cuts and yellowing bruises, causing Indigo to feel guilty about her mistaken pursuit of Ronald Spencer-Cooper, which had only prolonged her nephew's imprisonment.

Her remorse on that matter was enhanced by the presence of the country club owner's daughter Lily in the party. The younger woman's eyes drifted frequently to her boyfriend, like a hen checking to make sure a troublesome chick hadn't strayed again. Indigo smiled to herself, thinking Lily might do very well for Alan. He needed someone who appreciated his good points but was willing to stand up for him.

"I'm glad everything came out alright," she said to the room at large.

Violet's eyes widened. "Isn't that taking humility a little far?" she asked. "I really didn't expect you to unmask the murderer."

Indigo gave her a look of complete surprise. "Vi, that's exactly what you wanted me to do."

Her sister blushed and glanced away. "I know, but I was distraught. I was asking too much of you. Too much, really."

"Well, the clues were there and I just followed them. That was all I could do."

"It's a pity the police didn't. Then poor Alan wouldn't have been sent to prison at all." Alan gave his mother a look of appeal, embarrassed by her fury on his behalf. She shook her head at him. "It's true, Alan. They didn't even find the diary."

"You're quite right, they should have found the diary," said Indigo. "But DCI Waters was the one who was anxious to clear the case up quickly. He didn't really allow his men to do a thorough job."

"Well, that's easy for you to say. You seem to have become quite friendly with that inspector."

Indigo opened her mouth to point out all the work George had done on their behalf, then decided there was no benefit in getting into a sisterly argument. To change the subject she turned to Lily. "How's your father doing?"

The young woman looked pale and drained, but she managed to raise a smile. "He's out of danger and there's not as much brain damage as they feared. They're going to send him to a specialist hospital for rehabilitation. They think he's lost some motor function and will need to learn to walk all over again." She gave a huge sigh. "There's a chance he won't ever be able to go back to playing golf."

Indigo gasped, forgetting she still suspected him of bribery. "That must be awful for him."

"I don't think it's sunk in yet."

"And what about the club? Is the route going to revert to the original plan?"

It was Alan who gave the answer in his usual hesitant manner. "They're talking about a compromise, Aunt Indie. They want to use the current lane and widen it on both sides. It means losing some of the woods, of course, but not enough to damage the special environments."

"Amy's fairies are safe then?" Indigo chuckled, wondering how that colourful young lady was doing.

He studied her seriously. "The road won't go anywhere near the pond now."

"And daddy won't lose the B course, not really. Just a strip of rough that won't make too much difference." Lily took Alan's hand in hers and held it tightly. "Of course, the traffic will be whizzing past the edge of the course, but apparently there are things they can do to provide a barrier and cut down the noise."

"That will please him."

The girl looked down at the carpet with an air of sadness. "I'm not sure he cares any more. When he started to understand things again, mummy told him how much it hurt her that he spent all his time at the club. He's promised to step back and spend more time with us." She glanced up at Alan. "And he's promised to butt out of his daughters' love lives." Alan reddened but said nothing.

At that, melancholy threatened to descend on the company, so Violet jumped up and offered hot drinks. There was a round of acceptance, so she strode across the room and out of the door.

Alan watched her go, then turned to Indigo. "Mum's become over protective since I got back. I hope she'd not going to keep it up."

She laughed at him. "Let her be, Alan. You just be worried about whether she's going to let you go up to university or not."

"The term's already started. I'm thinking of deferring for a year. I thought Lily and I might go travelling." He gave his girlfriend a look of mixed adoration and concern. "Once her father's home, of course."

Staring at him in surprise, Indigo wondered what his mother would think about that and chuckled. It looked like things had changed a lot more than she'd realised. Was her young nephew actually beginning to grow up?

A little over a week after the arrest of Derian Winslow, Indigo found herself in the same Nunsfield café where George Howard had given her the name of Taylor's neighbour. It was as quiet as it had been then, and George was sitting opposite her, staring at his coffee cup.

"So, did Ronald Spencer-Cooper bribe Winslow and Porter?"

He raised his head, hands resting on the table a few inches from the cup. "Now that's a very interesting question," he said. "Technically, it was the other way round."

She blinked her surprise. "You're not saying Winslow bribed Porter and Spencer-Cooper?"

"Leave Porter out of it, he's completely innocent. It was Winslow. He pushed Spencer-Cooper into a corner where he felt he had to reward him."

"I'm still not following."

He leant slightly forward, a light of amusement dancing in his eyes. "Winslow wanted to join the Country Club. He was willing to pay the joining fee, but the Members Committee didn't want him. They rejected his application twice and told him not to apply again."

She winced, recalling the man's sense of self-importance. "I can imagine how that went down."

"He told me he was deeply insulted by their rejection and determined not to let them have the last word."

"But how —"

"By what he calls networking. In his world if you want something from somebody you put them under an obligation first."

"Ah, I begin to understand. He *was* bribing Spencer-Cooper. He knew he was desperate to save the B course, so he moved the road for him."

George nodded, and stopped to take a mouthful of coffee. Indigo took the opportunity to sip her own drink, then continued the conversation. "It was still corruption, even if it was instigated by Winslow. Just because he didn't ask for money, doesn't mean it wasn't a bribe."

"Of course, and Spencer-Cooper knew that. He hated it. He told me he wouldn't have had anything to do with it if Winslow had asked him before getting the route changed."

"You've managed to speak to him?"

"He's back home. I went round yesterday and recorded an interview. He's not well enough to come into the station."

"Mm, I suppose once it was a fait accompli it did make it difficult for him."

"As long as nobody queried it, he could live with it. Then Taylor came round accusing him of bribery and that threw him into a complete panic. When Taylor was killed and Alan Sherman locked up for it, Spencer-Cooper thought the heavens were smiling on him. Talk about two birds with one stone. A dangerous foe and his daughter's unsuitable boyfriend disposed of in a single stroke."

She gave him a rueful look. "You can see why I thought he was the killer, can't you?"

"Of course. If we'd got onto the bribery aspect, I'd have thought the same."

"So why did Winslow try to kill him?"

"Because that final conversation with you caused him to crack. He knew you didn't buy his alibi, and being in the woods around the time of the murder looked bad for him. So he decided the only thing he could do was come clean about everything. The bribe, following Lily, lying. He was going to come to us and take his medicine. But, being a basically decent sort, he thought he ought to warn Winslow first."

She took another swig of coffee. "You know Lily knew he was there all the time, don't you?" He nodded, but didn't interrupt her as she thought through what had been said. Finally, she shook her head. "I can't believe all that mayhem came about just because Derian Winslow wanted to join Great Oxing Country Club."

He studied her, brows knit. "Can't you? Winslow may be extreme, but he's a typical narcissist. He thinks himself a

VIP. He was incredibly condescending when we questioned him." He gave an ironic laugh. "He only wanted to join the country club because it was attracting celebrities. He felt he belonged there and really was deeply insulted by their implied snub."

"I get that, and I'd understand it if he'd killed the people who voted against him, but why go for Peter Taylor? There was real rage in that killing."

"In his mind the Members Committee were nonentities with no real class. He'd already worked out how to influence Spencer-Cooper. On the other hand Taylor was the only person who'd ever successfully thwarted him and he was threatening to do it all over again. I think Winslow just lost it. You saw what he was like when he attacked Carol."

There was another long silence as they drank."There was a lot of thwarted ambition in this case," he said after a few minutes.

"Strange you should say that. There was a point when I felt swamped by all the ambition swirling around me. I'm not sure about it being thwarted, though."

"No? Stalled, perhaps. Nash's protest group fell apart, Butterworth made a complete mess of his bid, Eleanor Knight will suffer for H&G's lack of profit, and Spencer-Cooper's B course is never going to mean as much to him again."

Their cups were almost empty. What would happen now? Would he shake hands, walk away, and never see her again? Would he suggest they remain friends? She swallowed hard and tried to meet his eyes calmly. "Well, thank you for inviting me here to bring me up to date,"

He took a deep breath. "Actually, that's not the reason I asked you to come."

Her heart started to pound. Here came the final break. "Oh?"

He reached across the table and awkwardly took hold of her hand. "I acted rashly. I mean —" The other hand ran through his hair, pushing it into adorable little peaks. "Being in a relationship with you was a problem as far as the case was concerned, but there were other ways of dealing with it."

"I guess that was the easiest." She heard the wistfulness in her own voice and cursed the weakness. "You weren't fully committed to our relationship, were you?"

He released her hand and wriggled uncomfortably. "That's my problem," he said quietly. "Ever since the divorce I've found it hard to trust women. I guess I'm afraid of getting hurt again."

"I can understand that." His ex-wife had left him for another man after a two-year affair. He'd already explained what a bolt from the blue it had been. Especially since she'd taken their daughters with her. Indigo steeled herself to be kind. "One day you'll find someone —"

"I already have." He was sweating and a nerve was jumping in his temple. "Oh Hell, Indie, I've missed you. The moment I closed that door I knew I'd made the biggest mistake of my life. I love you. Can you forgive me? Give me another chance?"

It was the outcome she'd hoped for, but her mouth was so dry she couldn't speak. He looked concerned and reached out for her hand again. "It's too late, isn't it? I insulted you, broke our bond."

She shook her head and managed to squeak "No." Then gulped and said, "I mean yes." She jumped to her feet. "Let's get out of here and go somewhere private. Somewhere we can hold each other, and kiss, and apologise properly."

He rose from his seat and came round to her side of the table, taking her by the shoulders. "What's wrong with right here?" And the next moment, she was in his arms and his lips were descending to hers.

THE END

Printed in Dunstable, United Kingdom

79718342R00122